Let the Sauce Simmer

A NOVEL. NOT A COOKBOOK.

TIM DAVIS

LifeRich
PUBLISHING

LifeRich Publishing is a registered trademark of
The Reader's Digest Association, Inc.

LifeRich Publishing books may be ordered through booksellers or by contacting:

LifeRich Publishing
1663 Liberty Drive
Bloomington, IN 47403
www.liferichpublishing.com
844-686-9607

Cover design by Bruce Crilly

ISBN: 978-1-4897-3085-5 (sc)
ISBN: 978-1-4897-3086-2 (e)

Library of Congress Control Number: 2020915664

Print information available on the last page.

LifeRich Publishing rev. date: 10/26/2020

To my wife, the lovely Helene; my amazing daughter, Danielle; and my son, Sam – a chip off the old block. You have been listening to me talk about this book, curse this book, and promise to finish this book for so many years I lost count. Thank you for your support and patience. Now that it's finished you damn well better read it.

To my late mother, Adelaide. She spent many years teaching me how to be a good cook and a good person. I will never be nearly as good as her at either one. In my defense, she set the bar really high on both counts.

Prologue

In the 15 years beginning in 1900, three million Italians left their homeland for the shores of America as part of the "New Immigration," the surge of Europeans that consisted mostly of Slavs, Jews, and Italians. In 1907 alone, over a quarter of a million Italians came to America.

Unlike the previous generation of Italian immigrants, mainly craftsmen and merchants seeking a new market that might be intrigued by their unique goods and services, these "new" immigrants were, in contrast, farmers, peasants and laborers simply looking for steady work and any opportunity to prosper. Many of these settlers quickly learned the meaning of the age-old American metaphor that the grass is always greener on the other side. Within five years, as much as 50 percent of this group returned to Italy and became known as *Ritornati.*

The ones that stayed endured depressions and recessions, epidemics, and discrimination. Their children – those who came to America as infants and those born here soon after their parents arrived – experienced the same trials and tribulations, while also challenged with carrying the family name and enterprise to greater achievement. And, sometimes, merely to survival.

CHAPTER ONE

Lessa Donato

Lessa Donato had a grandson named Nick. She called him Nicky. Sometimes she called him Dennis or Joey or Vinny or Michael. Sometimes she called him Buster or Francis. But she never called him Rick. Or Ricky.

In her family there was, in fact, a Dennis and a Joey and a Vinny and a Michael. There was a Buster and a Francis. There was a Lucky and a Marco. Lucky's real name was Roseanne. She got her nickname because she was born on Friday the thirteenth. She didn't get her birth name until thirteen days later. Lucky was married to Marco, a part-time butcher and full-time prankster who accidently cut off the tip of his left forefinger juggling meat cleavers, just for laughs.

His last name was Marcantonio, so everyone assumed Marco was his nickname. It never came up, but Marco was actually his given name – he was born Marco Marcantonio – and disfigured digit notwithstanding, he characteristically displayed pretty good humor and bonhomie. There was a woman named Cloris Morris who came to the house on Wednesday afternoons to make gnocchi for Morelli's, Lessa's Italian restaurant, by twisting her crooked thumb into a thick, soft mixture of boiled potato, flour, egg, and cheese.

But there was no Rick or Ricky. So Lessa never called her grandson Rick. Or Ricky.

Lessa's extended family included an ex-con named Dominic DiLorenzo who did 20 years on a murder rap, and Christian Rosa, a handsome young man who could have had any woman he wanted, but for some reason never did. He was an anomaly in a traditional Italian circle, but he was by no means an outcast. Christian could cook, tend bar, cut hair, hem trousers, wash windows, and make homemade ravioli. Depending on his audience he could be old school or new wave, but either way he was resolute in his beliefs and people respected him for that, even if they did not always understand him. Christian was Lessa's godson, but other than that it was never discussed how he was related.

There was Angelo Nunziato – a bookmaking cigarette salesman who wound up dead in his Lincoln Mark IV near a dandelion field on Canandaigua Road on his way home from the Mare-Do-Well Racetrack. He went to the track every day, but not until he picked up his bets and vigorish at Morelli's and other stops along his tobacco route.

There were many others whose lives intersected at Morelli's over the years. They came and went for the most part, all with their unique foibles and stories, although some stayed to the end.

Lessa Donato couldn't always match names with faces, but if you were part of her family tree, no matter which branch, she could recite even the most intimate details of your life at any given time. She knew who your friends were and who their friends were – maybe not by name but by some association. She knew where they lived, where they worked, where they went to school, where they socialized, and who they socialized with. She knew what sports you played, although she did not know anything else about those sports. If she didn't know, she asked. Even if she knew, she asked, probably to make sure you weren't lying. Lessa knew things about people in her family that she had no way of knowing and no reason to know. She knew your secrets, and you knew she knew. It wasn't worth lying to her. The best you could do was keep your mouth shut, and hope she did the same.

One subject Lessa never broached was schoolwork. Maybe she just figured everyone was smarter than her, and that embarrassed her. She had virtually no formal education and would just as soon skip over the entire topic for whatever reason. She simply cared more about cold cuts than cold wars.

Lessa knew Carl Mickey, a Sergeant on the Geneva Police Department and one of her closest confidants. A stereotypical Irish cop who liked his whiskey neat and his steak cooked well, "Mick" - his friends called him - was Lessa's personal police blotter, so not only did she know everything there was to know about the people in her family, she knew all about the general comings and goings around the town. Nick first witnessed her influence sometime in his mid-teens when he was arrested briefly for a public disturbance after guzzling malt liquor and laying rubber in a park by a lake.

He had not yet been officially charged or even allowed to make a phone call when his grandmother barged through the front doors of the Geneva Police Station and rambled up to the sergeant's desk. She was in a hurry and in a pissy mood. Nick was not behind bars; he was sitting in a solitary metal chair near a worn-out vending machine whose only inventory was a single roll of Necco wafers that up to then had his undivided attention. He was still lightheaded from the beer and too far away to hear any part of the conversation, but it was clear to him that Lessa was doing all the talking and, inexplicably, Sergeant Mickey seemed contrite. An argument with Lessa never decided who would be right, only who would be left. Most of the time that was her. She spun around from the desk and walked to where Nick was sitting. She paused for a moment, which to Nick seemed like several minutes, while looking down on him, her gaze austere. Piercing. She grabbed him by the arm and whisked him out of the same doors she burst through just a few minutes before.

A taxi was waiting at the curb; Lessa didn't drive. She shoved Nick, still tipsy, into the back seat and climbed in herself just as the cab pulled away. Finally, she uttered her first words to him in her subtle Italian accent that was more a consequence of her upbringing than her birthplace: "Don't be stupid," she said. Only Lessa, Sergeant Mickey and the teenage boy were privy to the events of that night, and they were never discussed thereafter. As for the cabbie, he was racing through the curved streets like a Grand Prix driver, with no instruction from Lessa. Yet he knew exactly where he was going.

It was a Friday night and everybody in Geneva, including the driver, knew exactly where Alessia "Lessa" Donato was supposed to be - Morelli's Restaurant, in what was known as the "ass end" of the town. Bad location. Great food. The service was average, but familiar and warm.

Morelli's was her business and her home, and they were interchangeable. The restaurant and bar were in the front of the building, facing the rust-colored brick street – Lehigh Lane. Lessa lived in the back rooms and upstairs, most of which faced the Lehigh Valley Railroad tracks, with her younger twin siblings - Gus Morelli, an inveterate gambler and self-proclaimed thoroughbred handicapper; and sister Sofia Riotto, who preferred a prayer book over a cookbook, but still knew her way around a kitchen. They were equal owners of the restaurant. Lessa ran the kitchen, Gus ran the bar, and Sofia kept them from killing each other. She could also make a wicked apple pie.

Lessa and her husband Salvatore Donato had three children, including Edie, their oldest; Lucky (Roseanne); and their youngest, Robert. As a little boy, Robert wore only Buster Brown shoes, so everybody called him Buster. There was a fourth child who was stillborn and thereafter was simply known as "the baby." Edie and Lucky were grown and married and raising families in homes of their own, but not too far from Morelli's. Buster attended college in Wyoming and came home on holidays dressed like he was traveling with a rodeo.

Sofia had three sons – Ronnie, Vinny, and Michael Riotto – who also lived in the house on Lehigh Lane. Her husband, Geno Riotto, left the family and never came back after the youngest son – Michael – was born. No one ever heard from him after that. Gus was a confirmed bachelor, but he did his best to help raise Sofia's boys in lieu of their real father. For a time, the Donatos, the Riottos and Gus Morelli were the only permanent residents of 59 Lehigh Lane, but on any given day, week, month or year a band of transient relatives and acquaintances who were visiting, or just needed a place to stay, called Morelli's their home. The doors to the living quarters in the back of the house were never locked, so you wouldn't always know who had slept there that night until they showed up for breakfast. They always showed up for breakfast.

Lessa, Sofia and Gus had another sibling, Rocco Morelli, who died in 1943 at the age of twenty-eight when he was gored by a forklift while working at the local soft drink bottling plant on Hoffman Street. Rocco had just started that job to provide a steady income for his young family. He played the trumpet and conducted his own orchestra, which is how he planned on eventually earning a living. It was the era of "swing," and the country was smitten by the beats of the Big Bands - Duke Ellington, Tommy and Jimmy Dorsey, Benny Goodman, Chick Webb, Glenn Miller, Artie Shaw, Woody Herman. Rocco was achieving a certain level of popularity in dance halls and small theaters around the Finger Lakes region of New York State, and his family and followers believed it would be a short amount of time before he appeared on much larger stages.

Rocco was an Ellington devotee, a disciple. He studied Ellington's volumes of compositions - instrumentals, suites, symphonies, movie scores, ballets. He had the "Ellingtonia" style down pat but always with a unique twist of his own - maybe a slightly slower tempo or pace, or a punch at the beginning of a chord. When Ellington introduced vocals into his repertoire, Rocco began a search for a voice that would add the same breadth to his own orchestra. He auditioned men and women from Buffalo, New York in one direction to Schenectady, New York in the other. He traveled to Scranton, Pennsylvania when he heard about a young bar room baritone, and all the way to Detroit, Michigan to hear a silky crooner that one of his co-workers at the soda plant told him about.

Rocco was a musical wunderkind not just because of the way he played music, but also because of the way he heard music. When he auditioned all those people for his orchestra he did not hear the music the way he thought it should sound. This was an important time for music. The nation was recovering from the Great Depression. Americans were going back to work in droves thanks to the industrial necessities of World War II. People were working hard, and they wanted to kick up their heels after the whistle blew. The Big Bands provided a spark. When the music was right, Rocco could hear the optimism and inspiration; to him it was sentimental and romantic. It was never mundane and was universal in its appeal. Rocco heard all of that whenever he heard Edie sing. She was only fourteen, half his age when he died in 1943, but her voice implied a lifetime of involvements. She could sound like she was on top of the world in one song and down in the dumps in another.

Young Edie would run home from school whenever Rocco rehearsed on the bandstand at The Nines, a catering hall and dance club down the street from Morelli's that specialized in weddings and other large parties. Rocco would bring Edie up to sing a few songs and was amazed each time how naturally she stayed in exact tune with the band, and how she belted out the lyrics with profound sincerity. Several times a year one of the Big Bands would come through Geneva on the train headed toward New York City and stop for a hot meal and a real bed before taking the first train out in the morning. The owners of The Nines opened the ballroom on such occasions and put out tables of antipasto, sausage and peppers, rigatoni with giblets, roasted chicken, salad drenched in oil and vinegar, loaves of Italian bread, and cheesecakes with various thick compote toppings. In return, the orchestra would rehearse into the night for an invitation-only audience of certain local dignitaries, friends, and customers of the club. Rocco sat in with his trumpet and never skipped a beat. On one occasion he called Edie to the stage to sing Doris Day's "A Bushel and a Peck," and she brought the line at the food tables to a standstill. When she forgot some of the lyrics, she drifted starry-eyed into a soft, sweet hum like it was part of the song. With her wavy blonde hair and white, toothy smile, Edie's physical resemblance to Doris Day was remarkable.

Two weeks after Rocco performed that night – it was with the Benny Goodman Orchestra – he was killed in the bottling plant less than a half mile from The Nines. Goodman and his drummer, Gene Krupa, attended Rocco's funeral at Saint Thomas Aquinas Church in Geneva. After the mass, Goodman saw Edie standing on the curb waiting for a car to take her to Saint Patrick's Cemetery. It was a snowy March morning; Edie was shivering. Goodman gave her a hug and wrapped his white silk scarf softly around her neck. "You don't want to catch cold. You could lose your voice. No one would be happy about that," he whispered. That scarf remained in Edie's house for as long as she lived there.

Rocco Morelli left behind a wife, Helen, and a one-year-old son, Francis "Franky" Morelli. Edie became Franky's regular babysitter, and his favorite bedtime lullaby was "A Bushel and a Peck." Some thirteen years after Rocco died, Helen married an Air Force Captain named George, a good egg who had nothing to do with music or forklifts. When Helen and George relocated to a town outside of the Geneva school district, Franky moved in with Edie and her family on North Walnut Street until he finished high school and enlisted in the United States Marine Corps, serving in Korea. After his tour he moved to Palmyra, New York, on the other end of Seneca Lake, where he started his own family. Whenever he came back to Geneva, Edie's house was his first stop. She always told him the story of Goodman's white scarf. It was a story Franky eventually passed on to his own children.

Morelli was Lessa's maiden name, and the restaurant was named after her parents – Joseph and Josephine Morelli. They came from Italy and settled in upstate New York in the town of Geneva, an ethnic melting pot on the northwest corner of Seneca Lake, notably the middle finger of the Finger Lakes, in 1907 or thereabouts. They brought with them two-year-old Lessa and the twins, who had just turned one. Rocco was born in Geneva several years later. Lessa got her nickname when the twins started talking but couldn't say "Alessia." They called her "Lessa." It caught on.

Joseph spent his first twenty-five years in America working as a commissary foreman for the Lehigh Valley Railroad Company. By 1932 he had saved enough money to open a butcher shop at 59 Lehigh Lane, a very large brick building just over the tracks from the railroad depot. In Italy, Joseph earned his living curing meats, so it was said, and with that experience and the contacts he made at the commissary, the butcher shop seemed like a logical business decision. The early business took up a partial space on the bottom floor along with a kitchen and living area. On the top floor were all the bedrooms and a big open area that housed several different businesses over the years. It was at one time a seamstress shop, another time a hair salon. When the Mare-Do-Well track opened in nearby Canandaigua, Joseph started another side business: a sportsbook. He took some action on college football games and prize fights, but mostly he focused on the horses because of the buzz created by the new track. When the betting was light, he would run the bets to the track himself and take the vig, but when the betting was heavy, he laid off the wagers with another bookmaker to balance the action, usually in his favor. Either way, Joseph was good for the general health and well-being of the new racetrack. He had unimpeded access to the paddock - an area normally reserved for horse owners, trainers, jockeys, and stable hands. Rumor had it that once, after a particularly unlucky week at the track, Morelli's

Butcher Shop ran a special on ground chuck. The consensus was that Chuck made for a better meatloaf than he did a jockey.

The butcher shop didn't last long and not because it sold chopped meat of dubious origin. Joseph loved to cook. His dream was to own a restaurant. He thought of it as his destiny. However, those who knew him best said he was a much better butcher and bookmaker than he was a cook. In truth, history would bear out that the Morelli women down through the generations were much better cooks than their male peers.

In the spring of 1934, Joseph shut down the butcher shop and began transforming the space into what would become Morelli's Restaurant. He enlisted the help of his friend Dominic DiLorenzo, who traveled by boat from Italy to America with Joseph and Josephine, hopeful to earn steady wages as a carpenter. Josephine insisted that Dominic accompany them because, she believed, it would make the move easier for her and her husband. Joseph would have someone to help get the family situated while she tended to the children. Joseph and Dominic had grown up together and become very close over many years, but unlike Josephine, Joseph did not see the value in paying the expenses of another international traveler. After much convincing from the young mother, who, by the way, was quite content with her life in Italy, Joseph acquiesced. In Italy, Dominic did regular handy work and repairs on the Morelli home and meat store near Cento, a small farming and fishing village in the northern part of the country that was better known for the Renazzo meteorite that fell there in 1824. He hand-crafted a crib for the baby Alessia that was so unique and flawless, expectant mothers from one end of the town to the other pleaded with him to construct similar pieces for their own imminent arrivals. Alessia's crib was the last one Dominic would ever build. On the day the baby was born, he carved her initials and birth date on the inside of one of the crib's legs, along with the word "angioletto." *Little angel*. The etching was so tiny it would be virtually undetectable, even by a person that knew where to look.

Josephine felt that Dominic would be more useful in the event of any crisis, perhaps even more useful than her own husband. She also figured Dominic might have a steadying influence on Joseph should his ambitions exceed his means, not an uncommon occurrence for him.

A few weeks after the construction began, with the two men working practically around the clock, Josephine Morelli suggested to Joseph that they offer Dominic the small room upstairs in the very back of the house on Lehigh Lane. The floor in the room was so blatantly uneven you could feel yourself leaning as you walked through the door. It was still a more accommodating space than the room he shared with Luigi Rufo in a boarding house on Willard Avenue. Josephine explained to her husband that having Dominic walk back and forth to the job every day was too much of a strain on him, and that eventually he would tire of the work and ultimately be less productive. Joseph agreed and approved the move, although he didn't much care either way.

Dominic's room at Morelli's had a small cot covered with a rough, brown blanket; a tipsy nightstand; and a small lamp with no lampshade. The night stand had a single drawer and in that drawer Dominic, every night, would place his pocket watch and chain; a jackknife that he kept as sharp as a barber's razor and used to slice apples and whittle small pieces of wood; whatever loose change and crumbled currency he had; and a walnut or two. Throughout the day he ate walnuts that he cracked two at a time by squeezing them together in his right or left hand. Josephine made sure there were always walnuts in the house, and whenever she brought a new bag home from the grocery store, she would remind Dominic that his supply had been replenished. A fresh bag of walnuts always brought a smile to his face. Always.

Many years later Lessa's young grandchildren got such a kick out of delicately placing their favorite marbles in the doorway to Dominic's tilted room and watching them roll hauntingly to the far corner. Sometimes they would wager that whosever marble landed last had to remain alone in the doorway until Dominic's heavy footsteps could be heard lumbering up the stairs to the second floor. By then well into his seventies, Dominic was a round, elfish figure with hazy blue eyes and thin white hair. His lower lip hung well out in front of his top lip and he barely spoke a lick of English when he spoke at all. Mostly he just snarled in Italian. The children figured that if he ever caught them playing in his room, he would smash their heads together the same way he cracked walnuts.

CHAPTER TWO

White Hot Ice Pick

On Tuesday, July 9, 1935, the headline in the Geneva daily newspaper read: "Father of 4 shot and killed in row over card game here"

According to the story, the murdered "father of 4" was Alberto Grillo, 50, of 5125 North Genesee Street. The "here" referred to an alley off the west end of Lehigh Lane between the newly opened Morelli's Restaurant and a bakery owned by Martin Delano. The suspected shooter was Dominic DiLorenzo, forty-six. The newspaper account said that DiLorenzo shot Grillo four times at around nine-forty the night before, after the two men had argued over a card game or gambling debt in the back room of Morelli's.

But mystery surrounded the provocation for the shooting then and did for decades to come.

The same group of men - including regulars Delano the baker, Jerome Salucci, Joseph Morelli, Luigi Rufo, Donny Agotti and, of course, the suspect and the dead man - had a standing card game every Monday night since Morelli opened his butcher store a few years before converting it to a restaurant. They all argued on Monday nights. Not always the same two men, not always only two men. Some of the arguments turned into verbal scrums peppered with Italian curses and insults. Most of the men at the table concealed some form of weapon, most likely a blade or a pistol. Rufo, who delivered blocks of ice to local taverns and eating places in that part of town, kept an ice pick tucked in his right sock. He threatened the kids who chipped away at his refreshing blocks of ice on torrid August days that if he caught them, he would "stick a white-hot ice pick" in their eyes. How he would get his ice pick white hot, or why he would even need to, was uncertain. Nevertheless, concealed weapons were not unusual and generally caused no agitation among the card players. The ass end of Geneva did not have street lamps and was eerily close to the Lehigh Valley train tracks, home to a revolving pack of hobos, winos, migratory workers and other villainous characters who traveled from town to town by hopping one of the empty cars along the "Route of the Black Diamond." The route was named for the lustrous anthracite coal it hauled between Easton, Pennsylvania, and New York City. You never knew when an ice pick in your right sock would come in handy. White hot or otherwise.

Still, no one was ever killed over a card game in Geneva. In fact, the Grillo shooting was the first homicide there in thirty years.

The card game had broken up about an hour before Donny Agotti telephoned the Geneva Police Station to report that he heard five shots and anguished cries coming from the direction of Morelli's. At the station, Sergeant Thomas Locke took the call. Agotti lived at 52 Lehigh Lane, across the street and two doors down from the restaurant. He was walking his dog after the card game like he did every Monday night as soon as he got home. When the shots were fired he was close enough to see what he anxiously described as orange flashes or flames in the dark alley. "The noise … like a gun." He formed a pistol with his thumb and forefinger and aimed it at the night sky. "It scare-a my dog."

Chief of Police R.T. Roth was on the scene in a few minutes with Sergeants Daniel Murphy and Douglas Chesen, Patrolman Stuart Hooks and Undersheriff William Stoddert. It was a rough neighborhood, but murder was still a showstopper. They found Grillo's body lying face down in a river of blood. An excited crowd was milling around the restaurant and entrance to the alley, and a few of the more curious entered the passageway to get a better look until the police came and chased them away. Several bystanders, upon questioning, corroborated Agotti's account that five shots had been fired, even though only four struck the victim. That was confirmed later that night when County Corner Richard Labriola conducted an autopsy at the Luhmann Undertaking Establishment on Pultney Street, where the dead man was taken by ambulance. Three bullets entered the body through the front and one through the back. Two passed completely through the body and two remained in it, one in the chest and one in the abdomen. One of the bullets that passed through the body was found lodged in the brick wall of the Delano bakery. Grillo died within a few minutes after the shots were fired, it was reported.

As the police reconstructed the shooting, they believed that Grillo walked out of the restaurant first and was followed by DiLorenzo. In the alleyway, DiLorenzo stood close to Grillo and fired three shots, then a moment later two more. This was the testimony of nearby residents who heard three shots then cries for help and two more shots. The general theory was that the fourth shot was fired as Grillo turned away, not yet mortally wounded, and the fifth shot missed altogether. The final bullet was never found. Again, the general theory was that the final shot was fired as Grillo was falling to the ground and DiLorenzo merely aimed too high. There were several signs of a physical struggle between the two men. The police reported that DiLorenzo and Grillo "were engaged in loud conversation just prior to the shooting." Grillo was holding a straight type razor in his right hand when he was shot and was still clutching the weapon as he laid on the ground. But there was no blood on the blade.

There was some confusion among the officers at the scene of the crime regarding the markings on the ground near the dead body. One set of footprints was observed on the left side of the body with the toes of the prints facing the body, and another set of prints, with the toes also facing the body, was found on the right side of the corpse. The prints on the left appeared to be slightly larger than the ones on the right, although the scuffle between the two men obscured the exact shapes and dimensions of the footprints. There were signs that both men held various positions while shoving each other around. Police Chief Roth concluded that the footprints could have belonged to either man prior to Grillo's collapse. Other footprints in the general vicinity of the fallen victim looked to be similar to the ones on the right and left of the body. In addition, some of the footprints could have belonged to the probing onlookers who entered the area before the police tape was installed. Officers Murphy, Chesen, and Hooks all agreed with their boss.

Grillo, a painter by trade, was survived by his wife, Peppa, and four children - Karen, Victoria, Madeline, and Joseph. He had been separated from Peppa for at least a year and was living in a boarding house on Exchange Street, in the center of town. He was born in Italy on May 8, 1885. Although DiLorenzo and Grillo were said to have been at odds over gambling for two days, the common implication was that their feud had been festering longer, about the same time Grillo left his wife. It was speculated, but unconfirmed, that DiLorenzo was courting Peppa after the split, which angered her husband. Up to that point the two men were said to have been friendly, but not necessarily friends.

CHAPTER THREE

Elusive Italian Carpenter

The headline in the daily Geneva newspaper on Wednesday, July 10, 1935 read: "Murder suspect evades police"

Police found DiLorenzo's car, a black sedan, in front of the restaurant, absent of any useful evidence of the shooting or leads to his whereabouts. Despite a police net thrown about the city and an alarm broadcast over the state police teletype system, DiLorenzo was still at large two days after the shooting. Lehigh Valley Railroad detective Mike Moran used a gasoline scooter to scour the territory along the railroad from Lehigh Lane to as far as Oaks Corners, clear on the other side of town, but without results.

Police Chief Roth issued a statement saying that his department had been working eighteen to twenty hours a day since the killing, "and a close watch is being maintained over every spot to which the suspect might possibly return. The search is citywide and not confined to any one section. A State Police net is also out for DiLorenzo and the alarm has been flashed to all sections of the city and surrounding cities to be on the watch for the suspect. Circulars with full details and a photo of the suspect have also been sent out."

Police broadcast the following description of the fugitive: "Wanted for murder first degree: Dominic DiLorenzo, Italian, has appearance of a German - 46 looks older – 5 feet 6 inches tall 170 pounds, stocky, blue eyes, gray or white hair, thin on top. May have small mustache. Has scar one-and-a-half-inch-long under point of chin, small scar in front of right ear, small scar on left temple, one-inch vertical scar center of forehead, scar in palm of right hand from base of thumb to little finger, one-half inch scar below left shoulder and back of space under arm. Was wearing dark suit and light cap. Occupation carpenter. Smokes Italian cigars. Assumed armed. May attempt to cross border into Canada or return to Italy. Any information please advise Geneva Police Department. Suspect is considered dangerous. Do not approach."

For the third day in a row - Thursday, July 11, 1935 - the same story once again consumed the front page of the local newspaper. On this day the headline boldly read: "Police baffled in killer hunt; DiLorenzo still at large"

The Lehigh Lane shooting was now three days old and reports conveyed a discrete sense of urgency on the part of District Attorney Gregory Sieferd, who told reporters he believed that DiLorenzo, "the elusive Italian carpenter," suspected in the fatal shooting of Grillo, "may be hidden by friends here in Ontario County, possibly even in Geneva," and that with Geneva police, state troopers of the Canandaigua substation and all available deputies cooperating in the search, "the suspect's whereabouts will eventually be discovered."

Sieferd, a bookish man whose glasses were far too large for his small, pointy nose and low forehead, was agitated by all the commotion this case was creating. He took particular exception to the morning's news that the search for DiLorenzo had police "baffled." Given their lack of experience in hunting down "armed" and "dangerous" fugitives, he thought the Geneva police were conducting a considerably tactical search. But what really pissed him off was that DiLorenzo fled in the first place and made all this work for everybody during the dog days of summer. Sieferd thought he should be on his boat on Seneca Lake fishing for trophy trout, or on the golf course kicking his ball out of the rough, or, at most, shaking down traffic violators and public drunks. But he figured a successful capture, indictment and conviction would better his chances in the next Geneva mayoral election. Sieferd long fancied himself as Grand Marshall of Geneva's Memorial Day parade, one of the most extravagant in Ontario County, even though the closest he ever came to die in military action was the time he burned the roof of his mouth on a sip of black coffee at his nephew's West Point graduation in 1933.

"When I get this asshole wop in my courtroom I'm gonna have his dago dick sliced off and stuffed in his own meat grinder," Sieferd said to County Corner Labriola during a brief adjournment in their witness inquiry in Geneva's City Hall. In all, they interrogated seven witnesses who were in the vicinity of the shooting on Monday night. Despite intensive questioning the inquest failed to bring from any witness testimony of seeing either man in the darkness of the alley while the shooting was in progress. Sieferd and Labriola could not even corroborate evidence that a card game had taken place on the night of the fatal shooting. No one was saying anything other than five shots were fired and cries of help were heard.

On Thursday, the dragnet focused on the section of the city in which it was first believed DiLorenzo might be hiding out - west of Lyons Road between Gates Avenue and North Street - with specific interest in Hogarth, Willard, and Prospect Avenues. The neighborhood was steeply slanted toward an Eastern European population, mainly first-generation immigrants from Poland, Russia, and Romania. The exception was the western half of Willard Street closest to the railroad tracks, where a significant population of Italians lived as many as four families to a house. DiLorenzo had shared the top floor in a house there with Rufo before moving into Morelli's during construction of the restaurant. He made the round trip walk every day north along the tracks from the west corner of Willard Avenue to the east corner of Lehigh Lane, then cut through about fifty yards of dense, overgrown weeds and bushes into the alleyway leading to Morelli's. The total trip covered less than a mile and took the pudgy DiLorenzo about sixty minutes on a good day. The evening trip back to Willard Avenue took a little longer because he had to negotiate the railroad tracks and ties more tenderly under the night sky. The search team figured he might be hiding in a house in the neighborhood. The houses were all at least two stories tall, and some were four stories. They had basements and attics and lots of nooks and crannies that could easily conceal a portly fugitive from plain view and even cursory searches. It was also plausible that DiLorenzo could be hiding in the thick trackside foliage somewhere between Willard Avenue and Lehigh Lane, with friends fetching him food and supplies in the dark of night.

Finally, on Friday, July 12, 1935, four days after the deadly shooting in the alley near Morelli's restaurant, the headline in the daily

Geneva newspaper read: "DiLorenzo captured last night – charged with murder first degree"

According to police reports, patrolmen Roger Ray and Richard Stapleton made the arrest at about 9:30PM Thursday night, after staking out the house at 29 Willard Avenue, where DiLorenzo roomed with Rufo before he moved in with the Morellis. The officers had taken a position on the back porch with the doors between them and the inside of the house left open. Other residents of the boarding house came and went but none even remotely resembled the fugitive's description.

When officer Ray investigated a noise at the front of the house, he noticed the cellar door was open and saw DiLorenzo charging up the cellar stairs carrying something in his right hand. Ray blinded him with the beam from his flashlight and drew his revolver. "Stop right there and put your hands in the air. Do it now!" the officer shouted. It was the first time in his fourteen years on the force that Ray pulled his gun in the line of duty. He yelled to his partner, "I got him … in the cellar … get the fuck over here … I think he's gotta fuckin' gun."

Stapleton came running, his pistol drawn and cocked. They trained their weapons on DiLorenzo as he continued up the cellar stairs to the front room of the house, where they cuffed him and notified the station. Ray was relieved. Stapleton was disappointed. Stapleton took DiLorenzo by the arm, led him outside and stuffed him in the back seat of a patrol car. Ray took the wheel and they headed downtown with the siren wailing. Soon, two other squad cars approached from the rear, their sirens also screeching, and within a few minutes the procession arrived at the Geneva Police Station on Castle Street, where a cordon of fellow officers was waiting on the steps.

After questioning DiLorenzo at the station, a very gratified and relieved D.A. Sieferd issued a statement that read, in part: "The law moved swiftly today to apprehend and charge Dominic DiLorenzo, 46, of 29 Willard Avenue with murder in the first degree in the pistol slaying of Alberto Grillo, 50, of 5125 North Genesee Street, in an alley off Lehigh Lane on Monday night. It was certainly a fine piece of work on the part of officers Ray and Stapleton to subdue and restrain this very dangerous fugitive. As District Attorney, I want to express my appreciation to them, and in this connection the same holds true for the entire Geneva Police Department. It was a fine example of modern methods of investigation and utilization of intelligence techniques in cooperation with State Police and county authorities."

As usual, District Attorney Sieferd was full of shit. He glamorized the details of the capture to curry the favor of the Geneva Police Department, whose endorsement he would seek the following year in his run for Mayor. Not to mention, his version of the facts made for much better press, perhaps even a book someday, he figured. But the reality of Thursday night's capture would come out in the trial when the milquetoast Officer Ray took the stand and swore to tell the truth and nothing but the truth under cross examination by Christopher Cappadona, DiLorenzo's court-appointed attorney. Cappadona, who was selected to represent the accused man because he could understand and speak Italian at a basic level, attempted to dispel the image Sieferd had drawn of DiLorenzo as "a hostile and desperate fugitive who was planning an elaborate escape back to Italy." His version was that on the night of the capture, the stocky little Italian carpenter was not "charging" up the cellar steps in the Willard Avenue house at all; he was staggering. He was not holding a gun in his right hand; he was carrying a near empty bottle of Lambrusco. Truth was, DiLorenzo was stone cold drunk, and the only trouble Ray and Stapleton had "subduing and restraining" him was keeping him from falling back down the stairs. He had been hiding out for almost three days in the same cellar where Luigi Rufo made his own wine and hung his homemade salamis to dry. There was also a curtain of hot red peppers strung vertically in separate strands of twine that, when completely dried, would be crushed into flakes and sprinkled on macaroni and soup. Behind that curtain of long red peppers was where DiLorenzo hid from the police on the first night they searched the house.

As for the "modern methods of investigation and utilization of intelligence techniques" that Sieferd praised in his statement, Ray and Stapleton were not actually "staking out" the house on Willard Avenue because of a tip that DiLorenzo might attempt to flee back to Italy, and would likely need certain possessions from his room, even though that's what they recorded in the department's movement log. By now it was common knowledge that DiLorenzo was living pretty much full time at Morelli's, and besides, a thorough search of the house at 29 Willard Avenue on the night of the killing already proved fruitless. They were there because they each needed seven hours to start earning overtime, thanks to the mandatory double shifts since the shooting on Monday night. They figured this was as good a place as any to put in the time given the wine cellar and charcuterie at their disposal. As Ray was heading toward the cellar to slice off another link of dried sausage – and not to investigate a noise he heard coming from that part of the house, as he originally told Sergeant Chesen – DiLorenzo, thinking all the residents of the house would be sleeping, was climbing the stairs to get to the first-floor bathroom. Ray was taken completely by surprise to see the suspect a mere three stairs below him. He fumbled for his revolver, and had DiLorenzo been armed, Ray might have never seen a nickel of that overtime. The only casualty that evening was the back seat of the squad car. DiLorenzo never made it to the first-floor bathroom at 29 Willard Avenue.

CHAPTER FOUR
Beauties and Ball Players

Labriola - the Coroner - and Sieferd - the District Attorney - continued their inquest on July 13 and 14. Among others they questioned Guy Aquino, of 300 North Genesee Street; Paul Diorio of 134 North Genesee Street; Emile Tibaldi of Border City; and Dom Domico of 13 Avenue E. Nevio Leone, a Phelps, New York farmer, was also brought in for questioning. It was alleged that on the night of the shooting Leone gave DiLorenzo a change of clothing, although he later denied to county officers that he had seen the accused slayer. Leone could have been charged with aiding and abetting a criminal, and might have done some hard time, had DiLorenzo not swore under oath that he broke into the house in Phelps and stole the clothes while Leone was out for the night. All of these men and several others, including the suspected shooter and his victim, were part of a retinue that may or may not have been acquainted in the old country, but who had come to be familiar since their emigration to the U.S. They were mostly tradesmen that worked independently for daily wages or in collaboration to improve their own lots. They were electricians, carpenters, plumbers, masons. They washed windows and patched roofs at perilous heights with no harnesses and ladders that were missing more rungs than not. They did what they had to do to earn their way, and whatever they did they did very well, and with great pride.

They played cards and dice, they drank a lot of wine and whiskey, and they talked about baseball, especially about their beloved New York Yankees. Except for Leone, the farmer, who serendipitously became a diehard Pittsburgh Pirates fan. In 1875, tobacco manufacturers began inserting trading cards to stiffen cigarette packaging and advertise their brands. Some of the cards depicted popular and beautiful actresses. These cards were known as "beauties." Other cards featured images of Indian Chiefs, and some presentations were of prize fighters. But the most popular and widely collected cards were of baseball players. Louis Leone, Nevio's uncle and godfather, and a life-long chain smoker, didn't care much for sports – although he did keep a "beauty" or two at his bedside – so whenever he remembered to withdraw a baseball card before crushing and discarding an empty pack of Lucky Strikes, he passed it along to his nephew. One of the cards featured Honus Wagner, an all-star shortstop for the Pittsburgh Pirates. Under normal circumstances, Nevio would have dispatched the non-Yankee card in a game of "topsies" or "leansies," or clamped it to the spokes of his Hibbard bike with a wooden clothespin to emulate the sound of a motor. He might have traded it for a Yankee player in very low demand. Nevio was younger than the other men in his group by about ten years and preceded them to America by several years to work on the family farm with his Uncle Louis, who had no children of his own. As a boy, Nevio collected baseball cards, he played with them, he traded them and like any ardent fan he studied them, sometimes with a magnifying glass to clarify the tiny print. When he discovered that Wagner was born on February 24, 1874, the same day twenty-one years before he himself was born near Naples, Italy, the card earned a place in the shoe box that he kept under his bed. He followed the shortstop's career as he blossomed into a perennial league leader in all offensive categories and a fearless middle infielder. On June 9, 1914, Nevio - then twenty years old - took a train to Philadelphia to see the Pirates play the Phillies at the Baker Bowl and was in the stands when Wagner became the first player in modern baseball to get three thousand hits. The milestone was a double off Philadelphia's Erskine Mayer, making Wagner the only player in baseball history to smack his three thousandth hit off a twenty-game winner.

Wagner played Major League Baseball for twenty-one seasons from 1897 to 1917, almost entirely for the Pittsburgh Pirates. He won eight batting titles and led the league in slugging six times, and stolen bases five times. Wagner was nicknamed "The Flying Dutchman" due to his superb speed and German heritage ("Deutsch"). He was inducted into the Baseball Hall of Fame in 1936 as one of the five charter members, receiving the same number of votes as Babe Ruth and trailing only the legendary Ty Cobb. Cobb himself called Wagner "maybe the greatest star ever to take the diamond."

But for all the accolades and awards bestowed upon him by contemporaries, fans and historians, Honus Wagner's real worth would not be truly appreciated until several decades later, long after he retired from baseball in 1917, and long after he died in 1955.

CHAPTER FIVE
Ugly Face

DiLorenzo's arraignment took place on Monday, July 15 at 9AM, and at approximately 9:02AM City Judge Thomas A. Kane denied Cappadona's motion to dismiss the first-degree murder charge against his client. The attorney claimed that the evidence introduced failed to show any deliberation or pre-deliberation, and that the crime which DiLorenzo was charged with was justifiable homicide. It went over in court like a loud fart at Sunday mass. Even DiLorenzo, who barely understood any English at all let alone legal mumbo jumbo, rolled his eyes at his attorney's suggestion.

Events leading up to the shooting and subsequent discovery of the dead body in the alley off Lehigh Lane came to bear from the testimony of about a dozen witnesses during the investigation's due process and Grand Jury hearings, as well as from the recollections of DiLorenzo himself in statements he made to Police Sergeant Chesen in the presence of a few other officers at the time of his incarceration.

After defeating an attempt by Cappadona to force Chesen, under court order, to produce the stenographic record of DiLorenzo's statement, District Attorney Sieferd directed the officer to describe in detail most of what the defendant told him immediately upon his arrest. Chesen said that DiLorenzo's statement related to meeting with several men in Morelli's restaurant on Lehigh Lane Sunday after the outboard motorboat races on Seneca Lake. They discussed the races, and finally Grillo suggested cards and they started to play. Some discussion over play between Grillo and DiLorenzo arose. Chesen said that Grillo made a suggestive motion with his hand and arms, and DiLorenzo responded. Ralph Sigmon, another witness the night of the shooting, said the defendant bought several drinks for others in the group, but did not buy any for Grillo.

According to the defendant's statement and others present that night at Morelli's restaurant, Grillo had several drinks and left the restaurant a few paces behind DiLorenzo. When he caught up to DiLorenzo in the alley outside of the restaurant, Grillo asked why he was not included in the round of drinks bought for the others. Testimony indicated that DiLorenzo's only reply was to the effect: "ugly face." *Brutta faccia*. Other witnesses testified that the snub was not the reason, or the only reason, for the ruckus. The two men then exchanged a few other words, possibly that they settle their differences on the other side of the railroad tracks, but DiLorenzo declined and they remained in the alley where the shooting took place. DiLorenzo told police that he didn't remember how many shots he fired, but that "I kept shooting." *Ho continuato a sparare*. After Grillo went down, DiLorenzo picked up what he thought was his own hat from the ground but discovered it was Grillo's hat, so he threw it on top of the bleeding corpse, retrieved his own hat and fled. DiLorenzo was rarely seen about town without his soft, floppy, gray speckled newsie cap that fit his bulbous head like it was sewn to his scalp. He was not concerned about leaving any evidence; he only wanted his cap to be back on his head.

Chesen identified the newsie cap removed from DiLorenzo shortly after his arrest and described two "roundish" blood stains on the top of the cap. He restated DiLorenzo's testimony that the cap fell from his head during the scuffle with Grillo, and that some of Grillo's blood must have reached onto the cap as it laid on the ground. There were also blood splatters on DiLorenzo's shoes when he was taken into custody. The officer explained how DiLorenzo had retraced his route from the scene of the shooting to Phelps, where he exchanged his pants and shirt at the home of Leone – but kept his hat and shoes - apparently remaining just ahead of the manhunt.

District Attorney Sieferd and defense attorney Cappadona indulged in considerable squabble during the hearing over the question of how Sergeant Chesen determined that DiLorenzo committed murder in the first degree. "I based my conclusions on information obtained by examinations conducted at the scene of the crime, and by statements made by the defendant himself," Chesen told the lawyers. Cappadona argued, to no avail, that DiLorenzo was too intoxicated at the time of his capture to offer any lucid reenactment.

The headline on page one of THE DAILY ADVANCE, a Canandaigua, New York newspaper, on Friday, October 25, 1935, read: "Indictments expected today in DiLorenzo case"

"The case of Dominic DiLorenzo, 46, of Geneva, charged with murder, first degree, moved closer to trial this morning when arrangements were made in Supreme Court here before Justice

Benjamin B. Monahan, of Rochester, New York, for the drawing November 12 of a jury for that action. Justice Monahan directed that the case be brought to trial during an adjourned term of the Supreme Court in Canandaigua on December 3. DiLorenzo is charged with the fatal shooting of Alberto M. Grillo, whose body was found lying in an alley adjoining a Geneva restaurant on the night of Monday, July 8."

DiLorenzo pleaded not guilty and was remanded to the Ontario County Jail until Wednesday morning at ten o'clock at the request of his attorney. Cappadona sought the adjournment to prepare for motions with reference to the murder indictment.

Despite all Cappadona's evidential ambiguities, innuendos, and equivocations, intriguing as they may have been, the DiLorenzo Grand Jury hearings commenced promptly at 10AM on Tuesday, November 5, 1935 at the courthouse in Canandaigua. The first witness for the prosecution was Joseph Morelli, who testified that the two men were at the bar in his restaurant at 59 Lehigh Lane for a short time before the shooting took place, but he fervently denied they had argued there on Monday night or had even conversed. He further stated under oath that no cards were played while either DiLorenzo or Grillo were present at the same time in the restaurant, and because he was inside his place of business, he did not hear the shots that were fired in the alley.

Denial of card playing in the restaurant on the Monday night of the shooting also came from Morelli's son Rocco. He told of hearing at least two shots and seeing the bursts of flame from the gun in the darkness of the alley from a position on the porch of the restaurant, and said he brought his father inside for fear that a stray bullet might strike him.

At least half dozen witnesses called by the prosecution gave testimony that there was no card game at Morelli's that night, and later, under oath, the police officers who took the initial statements from witnesses on the night of the shooting would admit that it was a "probability," or "assumption," that a card game was in progress, and not a certainty as they originally reported. The group had merely assembled at the bar after the Seneca Lake boat races to talk about the day's events and settle their wagers. It was testified that DiLorenzo did in fact buy the first round since he was the big winner at the races, and that he did in fact exclude Grillo from his good will. As for the alleged argument, whatever harsh words were exchanged between the two men took place outside of the restaurant and not within earshot of anyone else. Only two men knew the cause of the rift that led to the shooting, and neither one was talking.

The hearings ended on November 16, 1935 - eleven days after they started - when DiLorenzo, originally indicted for first degree murder, was allowed to plead to the lesser charge of murder in the second degree, a deal, he was promised, that would spare him from spending the rest of his life in prison with no chance for parole.

Sieferd realized there would be a question of fact for a jury regarding the necessary degree of deliberation constituting a first-degree offense, and told the court in agreeing to the plea that he believed he had developed a "technical case." In his decision he wrote, "Although there is no doubt that bitter feelings existed between DiLorenzo and Grillo, and that the defendant was in fear of his life, I have no eye witnesses to the shooting and feel that it is not up to me to oppose his plea of guilty to a second degree murder count."

In regard to his study of the Grand Jury, which had earlier returned the first-degree indictment against DiLorenzo, Justice Monahan said that while the circumstances constituted such a crime, a jury might feel more justified in rendering a second degree murder verdict.

Monahan lived in Victor, New York, near Rochester, and was not at all interested in anything that happened in Geneva, not even murder. "A real ethnic shithole," he would say over drinks at the Oak Hill Country Club in Rochester before and during the trial. "One asshole Italian shoots another asshole Italian and I'm supposed to give a rat's furry ass? Screw that."

In 1956, when Cary Middlecoff beat the great Ben Hogan for the U.S. Open Golf Championship at Oak Hill, then-retired Judge Monahan was in the gallery on the final Sunday. He was heard to say, "This Mississippi redneck shouldn't even be allowed to caddy for Hogan." Middlecoff was from Tennessee; he played golf at the University of Mississippi and in 1939 became that school's first All-American golfer.

Just like it didn't make a difference to Monahan whether DiLorenzo was guilty, or whether he should spend the rest of his life in prison versus twenty years or twenty minutes, he gave no mind to the fact that Emmett Cary Middlecoff, in his fifteen-year career on the PGA Tour, had forty wins, tenth all-time, including the Masters and two U.S. Opens, all despite having one leg slightly shorter than the other. The Judge died on April 1, 1957 when he was struck by lightning on the eighteenth hole at the Oak Hill Country Club. He was sixty-eight. Exactly six people attended his funeral; they were all immediate family members.

As for Cappadona, the defense attorney, he had heard enough from his client and witnesses to know that he was a far cry from being a skilled enough litigator to win this case in a trial by jury, so he was quick to convince DiLorenzo to accept the second degree deal. The card game allegedly at the center of the dispute between DiLorenzo and Grillo did not, as first thought, take place on the Monday night of the shooting. It was the day before, on Sunday night, while the men were playing a game of cards known among Italians as Briscola. An argument ensued in which insulting gestures and words were passed back-and-forth. DiLorenzo, as best any of the witnesses could make out, called Grillo a "*Ratto*." DiLorenzo told Grillo that if he didn't kill him, someone else eventually would. Both men had a lot to drink and the dialog between them was a confounding mix of Italian and broken English, which Judge Monahan quickly pointed out would be inadmissible to a jury. Neither attorney made an effort to question witnesses as to why a drink, or even two, would be the cause of a fatal dispute among two men who at one time were known to be friendly. One of the witnesses, Tommy Burkle, told a reporter for the local newspaper that had been covering the case closely, "It was open and shut – the guy shot him in the alley, ran, got caught and never really denied what he did. Murder's murder. Who gives a crap about motives?" Nonetheless it was a question that lingered among the locals for years after the trial.

So, it was confirmed that on Monday night, July 8, DiLorenzo carried his gun, a thirty-two-caliber pistol, to the restaurant. After a drink he was about to leave when Grillo accosted him and said he wanted to talk. The two men wound up in the alley where the argument grew more heated. DiLorenzo drew his gun and fired five times, although he was a bit hazy about the exact number. He said he and Grillo tumbled and fell over after the first shots and he did not know whether he fired again while the tussling was in progress or afterwards.

After the slaying, DiLorenzo fled up the tracks of the Naples branch of the Lehigh Valley Railroad and lost his bearings in the vicinity of

Mason Street near the hospital. Once he realized where he was, he made his way to Phelps where he obtained some clean clothes at the home of his friend, Nevio Leone, and changed in the bushes near the barn. He removed the final bullet from the six-shooter, threw it as far as he could, and then stomped the pistol into the mud.

On November 16, 1935, Dominic DiLorenzo was chained around his waist, ankles and wrists and waddled out of the Ontario County Court House in Canandaigua and into a freshly painted Department of Corrections bus that would deliver him to Attica Prison, where he would serve his term of twenty years to life. The distance between Canandaigua and Attica, New York was about fifty miles, consuming mostly corn fields and cow pastures. The dry and dusty road heading west, Route 20, was always bumpy regardless of the weather. Usually by the middle of November this entire track would be knee deep in snow, but the remnants of a rare upstate New York Indian Summer permitted the D.O.C. bus to rattle toward its destination at a top speed of thirty-five miles per hour.

Gazing out the bus window for all of the fifty miles, DiLorenzo had ample time to consider his fate, and reflect upon what brought him to this moment. Throughout his trial he exchanged glances with Joseph and Josephine Morelli, who sat together a few rows behind the defendant's table. Joseph missed some days of the proceedings to tend to the restaurant or visit his friends in New York City, but Josephine was in the courtroom every day, always arriving before the trial participants and not leaving until DiLorenzo was ushered out of the room in shackles and back to the Canandaigua jail. On the days when Joseph did not accompany Josephine to the courthouse, she would hitch a ride with the lawyer Cappadona. They sat silently on the morning drive. Josephine's English was not that good to begin with and she had a natural distaste for lawyers besides. Mostly she figured DiLorenzo was going to prison so what else needed to be said? The D.O.C. bus driver took her back to the restaurant after the trial on those days, and in appreciation she would serve him a big dish of spaghetti and meatballs, a salad with oil and vinegar, and a few slices of crusty Italian bread. No charge. She could have driven back to Geneva with Cappadona, but she would rather take the D.O.C. bus with a driver who had no opinions on anything, save for the homemade meatballs - he thought they had too much garlic but were still the best he ever had - and he never said a word about them, or the trial, to Josephine.

Dominic DiLorenzo had worked his entire life with wood, even when he was only whittling with his pocketknife. He made furniture for homes and wooden animals so small they would fit in hollowed out walnut shells. He built a bar and a dining room from scratch. He sawed, sanded, and carved without blueprints or renderings. And now he would be spending twenty years or more behind steel bars and walking on cold, concrete floors. No tools. No wine or homemade sausages. No Joseph. No Josephine. The only improvement in his life might have been a firmer bed and a softer blanket than what he had in the room upstairs at Morelli's.

CHAPTER SIX

Road Trips

On November 23, 1955, Lessa Donato, who was then fifty years old, boarded a Greyhound Bus on Exchange Street in Geneva, New York for the sixty-mile trip almost exactly due west on the newly opened New York State Thruway to the town of Batavia, New York. At Batavia she hired a local driver to take her eleven more miles southwest to Attica, New York, right up to the visitor's gate at Attica Prison. Her mother, Josephine, had made the trip to visit DiLorenzo every year on or around November 23 since his incarceration in 1935. If a Visitor's Day did not fall on November 23, Josephine would make the trip on the nearest day before November 23, but never after. On three occasions since 1935 did Thanksgiving – which was always a visitation day at Attica – fall on November

23 – 1939, 1944 and 1950. On all three of those dates Josephine made the trip to the prison to visit with Dominic and would not allow the family's Thanksgiving meal to be served until she returned home in the evening. The restaurant was closed on Thanksgiving, so she would not be missed during the day. After her Attica trip in 1944, the idea of having the Thanksgiving meal later in the evening caught on with the entire family, and it became an annual tradition, that is for as long as the family celebrated together.

This was Lessa's first time to Attica. Josephine died two months earlier at the age of sixty-eight following a series of strokes. She grew increasingly weak toward the end and was confined to her bed in her last days. Just hours before her final breath she asked Lessa, her oldest child, to visit Dominic in her stead, specifically on November 23, which was his birthday, and happened to be an official Visitor's Day at the prison. Lessa and Dominic visited for the full one-hour allowance, although the conversation was cryptic and enigmatic for reasons beyond the language barrier. The old man barely spoke English and the younger woman's Italian was organic, obtained mostly from growing up in a near-exclusive Italian household. But by the end of the hour everything that needed to be said was said, and everything that needed to be understood was clear enough to both of them. Lessa left the prison in tears and muddled about her feelings. Dominic was stoic, as usual.

On February 17, 1956, Dominic DiLorenzo walked out of Attica Prison a free man. Terms of his parole required him to list a permanent residence in the state of New York. The day he was released he took the same route to 59 Lehigh Lane in Geneva that Lessa had taken when she left the prison a few months earlier, on November 23.

On the bus ride back to Geneva, Lessa had deep thoughts about her conversation with Dominic that day in Attica Prison's visitor area, but she was occupied by more than what transpired during the visit. In fact, the closer she got to home the more her attention turned to her oldest child, Edie, and to Edie's two young sons, Dennis and Nick. Nick was born on March 9, 1955 and was the new baby in the family. His older brother Dennis preceded him by seventeen months, and although he was too young to realize it, Dennis had simply become Nick's wing man. Lessa was looking forward to spending the entire next day with her family before she would have to take the giant turkey out of the oven and set the table for that evening's Thanksgiving meal. That would not be the case, however.

When Lessa arrived home from Attica that night she found Edie waiting for her in the back room off the kitchen at Morelli's, drinking coffee and smoking a cigarette. Before a word was spoken, Lessa knew in her bones that something was wrong. It was right around bedtime for Edie's two boys, and Lessa knew Edie always put them down for the night, never their father, who wouldn't know how to change a diaper even if it was his own. Also, Edie had her hair in curlers and covered in a net, which her Aunt Sofia, Lessa's sister, probably did for her in the beauty parlor over the restaurant. Edie's fingernails were also freshly painted. The family Thanksgiving dinner in Morelli's was never a hair-do-and-nail-polish occasion; it was more a day for flour-dusted cooking smocks and food-stained moppines. Edie was going somewhere, and her mother knew it. They were both uneasy.

That morning, as soon as Lessa left for Attica, Edie's husband, David, announced that he would be taking his family to visit his parents in Dublin, Ohio for Thanksgiving. He would borrow his father-in-law Sal's 1950 four-door Packard Super Eight sedan to make the seven-hour drive to the house he grew up in with his two brothers and two sisters on Briarwood Court, a waspy, upper crust neighborhood with Cadillacs parked in neatly paved driveways lined with scarlet and pink carnations. They would arrive at about three in the afternoon and his mother would have the turkey and all the trimmings on the seasonally decorated table in her formal dining room. The plan was to leave Geneva by 8AM, or as soon as David returned from deer hunting with his brother-in-law – Marco Marcantonio – and some of the other guys from V.F.W. Post 2670 on Seneca Street. Every year, on the first day of deer hunting season, the men would pack a couple of sandwiches and thermoses of coffee and meet at the Post at 3AM on the dot and drive to the thick woods out near Ramsey State Park to begin the hunt. In most years they would finish hunting, clean their kills, then watch TV in between naps for several hours while Thanksgiving dinner was being prepared.

That's where Lessa had a real problem. It wasn't so much that she would miss Nick's first Thanksgiving, and that it would be her first Thanksgiving ever without her daughter Edie. What really yanked her linguine was that her idiot son-in-law suddenly decided he would stay awake for almost twenty-four hours straight playing cards and hunting deer, and then drive his two young sons and his wife all the way to Ohio. When Edie went upstairs to take the rollers out of her hair, Lessa left the restaurant and walked determinedly for a half mile in the night air to the Poole house on North Walnut Street. She found David playing poker at the kitchen table with the rest of his hunting party and pleaded with him to cancel the trip until the weekend, or at the very least leave later in the day after a sound sleep. Lessa was being very reasonable, which was unlike her. David was being a stubborn prick, which was not unlike him. He reminded his mother-in-law that he would be driving to Ohio in the Packard, which was built like a railroad car and probably weighed as much. He told her his mother was very anxious to meet her new grandson, which was also her second after Dennis, and that she was expecting them for dinner, served in the Poole home in Dublin every Thanksgiving Day promptly at three in the afternoon. All of that was probably true, but what Lessa also knew about David was that he was a died-in-the-wool, white-bred mama's boy, and because of that there was no changing his mind. David Poole would do anything not to fall out of favor with his mommy.

Edie hitched a ride home with a Morelli's waitress and met Lessa at the front door as she was walking out, red faced. David nor any of his poker pals offered to drive her back to the restaurant, even though they all knew she didn't drive. Edie arranged for the waitress to drive Lessa home and she walked her to the car at the curb in front of the Poole house. Before their embrace ended, Lessa told Edie to stay awake during the trip. "Make sure that son-of-a-bitch stops on the way a few times to rest his eyes. Come by the restaurant on your way to the highway and I'll give you some sandwiches and pop to take with you. I'll be up. And call me as soon as you get there. Call me collect." Then Lessa got in the car and went home and right to bed. Given all the substance of that day – her visit with Dominic and the looming trip to Ohio – she barely closed her eyes at any point during the night. In the morning, as promised, she had a bag of sandwiches and several bottles of soda pop ready to load into the Packard. She also packed a large plastic container of Morelli's homemade meatballs and sauce for Edie to give to her in-laws. Alessia Donato would never visit anyone with empty arms. Nor would any of her children.

One other time, several years later and also on a Thanksgiving Eve, Lessa stormed out of Morelli's in the chill of night and walked to the Poole house to confront David. She had caught wind of a rumored affair he was having with a woman in Rochester, New York, where he was working at the time and supposedly spending a couple nights a week in a motel there to avoid the forty-mile drive back to Geneva.

What made this confrontation especially rousing was the fact that David's parents were visiting from Ohio for the holiday, and they had front row seats to the main event. Lessa caught everybody by total surprise and none of them – not David, not his father, not his mother – were prepared to offer any refutation or explanation. Edie was upstairs putting Dennis and Nick to bed. By now they had a sister, Vicki, and a baby brother, Joey, and they were already fast asleep. But the two oldest boys were wide awake, and they could hear every word of their grandmother's intemperate outburst. Edie was too ashamed to go downstairs and intervene, on whose behalf it could not be said, so she just laid in bed. Dennis and Nick may not have fully grasped the gist of the hubbub but based on Lessa's invective they figured their father did something really bad and that he was in deep shit for whatever it was. As Lessa left the house in tears, Dennis, wearing only his pajamas and slippers, ran down the stairs and out the front door without saying a word to anyone. Nick watched out of their bedroom window as Dennis took Lessa's arm and the two of them walked off into the frigid, dark night on snow-packed sidewalks heading back toward the restaurant. When Dennis returned to the bedroom he shared with his brother, the cold coming off his body gave Nick a chill, even though he was tucked tightly under the covers.

"Where'd you go?" Nick asked.

"None of your business," Dennis said.

"Why won't you tell me?"

"Because you're an idiot. Go to sleep."

The headline in the daily newspaper in Ashland, Ohio on Friday, November 25, 1955 read: "Six injured in holiday RT. 42 crash; four in one family"

According to the article, a head-on collision on Route 42 near the Richland County line Thanksgiving morning injured six persons, including four members of one family. One of the cars was destroyed by fire. A two-year-old boy in the car carrying the four passengers was the most seriously hurt. Another son, eight months old, escaped with bruises. The state Highway Patrol reported that cars driven by Vincent Daiken, 46, of Columbus, Ohio, headed northeast on Route 2, plowed head-on into the southbound car driven by David Poole, 25, of Geneva, New York.

The paper reported that a passing motorist, Hugh F. Lecky, Jr., of Springfield, OH, was credited with rescuing Daiken and his wife Shelly, 40, who both suffered broken legs and other injuries. Lecky also aided the four members of the Poole family. It was after he helped Davis Poole and his wife and older son from their wrecked car that he heard cries and discovered the infant son on the floor in the back seat. The Ashland post of the Highway Patrol would investigate the crash, which occurred about 1PM Thursday.

That investigation eventually revealed a more detailed account of the crash and its aftermath. Much of the testimony would come from Edie, who despite having her left leg attached below the knee by only strips of skin and some tendons, and blood coming from all sides of her head and face, was the only victim still conscious when help arrived, except for baby Nick.

The accident happened several miles southwest of Ashland, about where David picked up Route 42. They were five hours into the trip and less than a hundred miles from Dublin. The Daiken car could have been speeding as it approached the crest of a hill heading northeast on Route 42 in the right lane. David's car, which was probably speeding above the limit – Edie was always telling him to slow down – was cresting toward the same hill going southwest, when he decided to pass another car, the one driven by Hugh Lecky, in the left lane of the two-lane road. Before David switched back to the right lane, his car, and the one driven by Vincent Daiken, met head on at the top of the hill. The sound of the crash was so loud that people in downtown Mansfield, about eight miles away, thought a building had exploded, and motorists on Route 42 as far as fifteen miles in either direction could see a plume of dark smoke. At impact, the rear end of the Packard was lifted about ten feet off the ground and the car spun completely around and came to rest facing north, same as the Daiken car. All four tires had been blown off and the front of the car on the passenger side, where Edie was sitting, was sheered away, with only smoldering scraps of metal dangling from the frame. The entire front end of the Daikens' car, everything forward of the windshield, was unrecognizable. Most of it was smashed into the cab of the car and the rest disintegrated in the explosion. Flames were coming up from underneath both the driver and passenger sides of the car.

Lecky, who was taking his wife, Janet, and two-year old son, Rick, to visit his parents in Newark, Ohio, saw the crash from behind the wheel of his car and pulled off the road as close to the collision as he could without endangering his family. He had the presence of mind to open his trunk and grab the tire iron. The two crashed cars were about twenty yards apart. He ran to the Daikens' car first since it was in flames and was able to pry open the crumpled rear door on the passenger side with the iron. The impact of the crash pushed both passengers into what had been the back seat. Their legs were mangled and pointed in directions that defied anatomy. Lecky could see clearly and immediately that both of Mrs. Daiken's legs were badly fractured, and he could see bone but did not know to which leg it was attached. She was also bleeding from the abdomen and face. Mr. Daiken was bleeding from somewhere on his head or face, there was too much blood to see exactly where it was coming from, and his right leg was fractured near the knee. They were both unconscious. Lecky dragged them from the car to the side of the road, Mrs. Daiken first, without regard to causing further injury to their tattered limbs. He wasn't even sure they were alive.

While the rescue up to this point seemed like an eternity to Lecky's wife Janet, who was pacing fretfully roadside with her little boy as she watched her husband dash from car to car and from body to body, police and emergency reports would conclude that Lecky got both Mr. and Mrs. Daiken out of their burning car and to the side of the road in less than two minutes.

It was the middle of the day on Thanksgiving and there was not a lot of traffic on the road. Lecky was still the only one on the scene of the crash. As soon as he pulled Mr. Daiken safely away from the wreck, he rushed to the Packard. Edie, miraculously, was still conscious and clutching Dennis, who at the time of the collision was sitting in the front seat between his two parents. They were not wearing seat belts. Both David and Dennis were bleeding from their heads and faces and neither one was conscious, nor alive for all Lecky knew. Edie's left leg looked like it had snapped in two below the knee and she appeared to be delirious. Lecky did his best not to touch the shreds of raw flesh and jagged bone, as if it would bring her more pain, but he could smell gas all around him and knew that the flames from the Daiken car would soon ignite both wrecks.

By the time Lecky got David, Edie, and Dennis out of the car and to the side of the road, the Ashland Fire Department and other emergency responders had arrived at the site. Lecky was still tending to Edie, doing his best to calm her down. She was screaming, "My baby, my baby boy. He's in the car! Please!" Despite the efforts of Lecky and the emergency personnel to assure her that they in fact did pull "her baby boy" from the car, Edie kept screaming evermore frantically for them to "save my baby."

"We have your son. He's with us. He's OK," a fireman told her. They all assumed she was still delirious and heading into shock. Not until a responder who was working close to the Packard hear the faint cry of an infant and realize that Edie was talking about her eight-month-old "baby boy" Nick, and not his older brother, Dennis. The baby was lying in a bassinet that had fallen through the floor in the back seat and was now on the ground surrounded by the smoldering wrecked Packard. Within seconds after four firemen lifted him out safely, the car burst into flames. They handed Nick to his mother swaddled in the same blanket he had been travelling with, and she immediately passed out. The baby did not have a scratch.

CHAPTER SEVEN

The Heli Padre

In 1956, nearly a year to the day of the car crash in Ashland, Ohio, the twenty-five-year-old Hugh F. Lecky, Jr., a U.S. Navy Corpsman, was ordained as a minister of the Lutheran Church in America. In 1960 he became a U.S. Navy Chaplain. In 1961 he received the Navy Commendation Medal for helping to evacuate sailors from an exploding Nationalist Chinese tanker in Taiwan, where he was assigned to a destroyer that was visiting the port of Kaohsiung. And in 1966, Chaplain Lt. Cmdr. Hugh F. Lecky, Jr., then on duty with the United States Marine Corps., was named Chaplain of the Year by the Reserve Officers Association of the United States.

Lecky became known as the "Heli Padre" because he flew more than one-hundred-fifty helicopter missions with combat troops on air-borne assault strikes and medical evacuations. His only weapons were the Chaplain's medical kit that he wore on his left hip; a corpsman's bag on his belt; and an unflappable faith in the human spirit. His gangly build and boyish face belied his imperishable courage under fire. According to an article in the August 6, 1965 issue of the Windward Marine, published by the Marine Corps. Air Station in Kaneohe Bay, Hawaii, "Countless hundreds of U.S. Marines and Army of the Republic of Vietnam (ARVN) soldiers have been comforted or treated by [Chaplain Lt. Cmdr. Hugh F. Lecky, Jr.], a lot of them in landing zones so active it was difficult to breathe without inhaling lead."

The article also detailed the time when Lecky reached out of an airborne helicopter to lift a refugee child to safety. He did it without the person holding the baby realizing what was happening. When the child was lifted, two hand grenades were left in the person's arms; they had been hidden beneath the infant. Still holding the child, the Chaplain instinctively kicked the disguised Viet Cong soldier away from the helicopter, allowing Republic of Vietnamese soldiers to carry him away before he could detonate the grenades.

On July 8, 1965, Lecky became the first Navy Chaplain to be wounded in action in Vietnam, a distinction that would also make him the first Chaplain to be awarded the Purple Heart for service during the Vietnam War. The outpost at Ba Gia in Quảng Ngãif Province, South Vietnam, had been overrun by Viet Cong the day before, and retaken by ARVN soldiers the day Lecky arrived in a helicopter of the HMM-261 squadron assigned to evacuate the wounded. The "Heli Padre" was the only American medical person on the Observation Post (OP) at the time. He had conducted last rites for a helicopter pilot who was shot down, then reached over to his left hip and grabbed the medical kit. Lecky was administering first aid to wounded soldiers and civilians when a VC mortar round exploded sixty feet away and sent small slivers of steel ripping into his right leg. He stopped long enough to dress his own wound, then continued to aid the ARVN soldiers and civilians for another ninety minutes.

In his history of "**Chaplains with Marines in Vietnam 1962 – 1971,**" part of a series of functional volumes on the Marine Corps.' participation in the Vietnam War, Commander Herbert L. Bergsma, CHC, U.S. Navy, described Navy chaplains serving with Marines as "a vital partnership of fighting man and man of God which has been an integral part of the history of the Marine Corps. since its inception ...

... "In the field hospitals and on the line, the U.S. Navy chaplain in Vietnam could be found with the Marines who needed him most. His ministry and compassion extended into the villages, as well — as he sought to provide aid and comfort to all those victimized by the harsh blows of war ...

... "It was not unknown for a chaplain to brave intense fire in order to be at the side of a grieving infantryman who had just lost his best friend in combat. With skill and patience, he helped the survivor deal in human terms with the pain of inevitable — yet still traumatic — losses in battle, even while he comforted the wounded, the sick, and the dying."

It is not known whether Commander Bergsma knew Hugh F. Lecky, Jr. personally, or even if he ever heard testimony of Lecky's wartime heroics. Lecky may or may not have been mentioned specifically in the historical account of Navy chaplains. But it would not be hard to believe that Bergsma could have used Lecky as the inspiration for his rendering.

Nor can it be said that Lecky had seen any combat or even had any rescue training before that Thanksgiving Day in 1955 on Route 42 near Ashland, Ohio. Maybe he had no thought or ambition of becoming a chaplain at that time. But what can be certain is that if the car that David Poole passed on Route 42 that day was driven by a person of any less courage and obsession for human life, by any person not as selfless or fearless, or by any person less moved by the hand of God, there would probably have been eight dead people lying in the middle of the shredded, smoking metal, including two yet to be born. Both Edie Poole and Shelly Daiken, the passenger in the other crashed car, were two months pregnant. They would both give birth to healthy girls – Rose Daiken and Vicki Poole – within months after the accident.

Maybe Hugh F. Lecky, Jr., was moved by his experience on Thanksgiving Day in 1955 to further serve his country and humanity by bringing comfort to those ravaged by the horrors of war. And maybe God had sent him a reminder of why he was even there in the first place by projecting the mortar shrapnel into his right leg in Vietnam that day in 1965; ten years earlier it was Edie Poole's nearly severed left leg that he held together as he carried her from the wrecked Packard. Or he could have just wanted to honor his older brother, Richard, who was critically injured in WWII during the Bataan Death March in April 1942, in which thousands of Filipino and American prisoners were severely and physically abused while being transferred by the Japanese army from Mariveles, Bataan to San Fernando, Pampanga. However it came to be, Hugh Lecky had a calling and he embraced it at the ultimate cost. In his profile of "Chaplains with Marines," Bergsma wrote: "… A common bond of sacrifice linked the U.S. Navy Chaplain with the Marines he served. In this, the chaplain remained true to his heritage: Greater love hath no man than this; that a man lay down his life for his friends."

Hugh Lecky, the "Heli Padre," passed away in 1999 from cancer believed to be caused by exposure to Agent Orange while serving in Vietnam.

The accident on Highway 42 in Ohio in 1955 was not Nicky Poole's last brush with death. When he was six or seven or thereabouts, his Uncle Buster took him, Dennis, little Joey and a couple of his nephews from his wife's side of the family camping in a thickly wooded area near Honeoye Falls in upstate New York, although for what the children knew it could have been a different planet. It was desolate and dark and as they walked through the woods along barely defined paths over rocks and fallen branches, the only sounds they could hear were the crackling and crunching of dried leaves and twigs beneath their footsteps and the squawking birds above their heads. It was spooky; they stayed close. They came upon a clearing - a round patch of hard pan with the charred remnants of a campfire inside a small circle of rocks. They were not the first to inhabit this planet.

Buster was fresh out of a Wyoming college and fancied himself a cowboy. His faded dungarees rested just above the tapered heels of his boots. The silver, oval buckle on his thick leather belt was shiny with small embedded blue stones. He was bold legged because, he made clear, he paid his way through college working on a horse ranch.

When the group arrived at the camp site Buster told the youngsters to help unpack the supplies and set up the tents before they went exploring. He warned them not to go in the lake until he got there.

Nick, who was well known by now to be more rebellious than his older brother, immediately ventured into the water without an adult in clear view. Every single detail that took place in the next two to three minutes, even the paltriest, remained vividly clear to him throughout his entire life. He went out far enough that the water came up to his chin while he was stretched on his toes. He must have had his feet on some slippery clay that fell off into a deep drop. As he bobbed up and down trying desperately to keep his mouth and nose above the water line, Dennis and Joey laughed like hyenas, fortunately for him loud enough for Buster to hear. As Buster approached the shoreline to quiet the boys down, Nick could see the annoyed look on his face. Then Buster realized his young nephew was struggling to stay afloat. Nick always remembered exactly how his uncle sprinted toward the water and in a single motion took his wallet from the back pocket of his jeans and tossed it aside, never slowing his stride. He remembered exactly how Buster lunged into the water – a dive so flat he may have skipped once or twice across the calm, green surface. Nick remembered the exact fraction of a second when Buster disappeared under the water and he remembered precisely the next second when he felt the top half of his body being heaved above the water. He remembered his Uncle Buster towing him to the shore and pushing on his chest while the water spilled from the side of his mouth.

Nick remembered how he was afraid of dying and seeing parts of his short life flash in front of him as he was going under three, four, even five times, although there wasn't much to see and what was there was not overly impressive. Nick never thanked his uncle. But rarely did a day go by – particularly as he grew to a man and had children of his own – that he did not think about how close he came to die that day at the lake. And how it was Uncle Buster who made sure he didn't.

And he remembered what assholes his brothers were.

CHAPTER EIGHT
Doctor Peaches

Edie spent the next several months in a hospital in Ashland, Ohio. From the moment she arrived in the emergency room, doctors there held little hope her left leg could be saved. The major bone extending from the knee to the ankle had broken through the flesh in two places. Treatment options back then were limited. Limb salvage techniques used to remove bone and soft-tissue cancers and avoid amputation, had not yet been developed in the mid-1950s. Likewise, synthetic bone and cadaveric bone from a bone bank were not yet available. In Edie's case, some of the doctors at the hospital recommended amputation above the knee.

A young orthopedic surgeon from Steubenville, Ohio, Dr. Alfonse Siklosi, felt differently. Flying in the face of conventional medical wisdom at the time, Dr. Siklosi performed bone graft surgery using bone harvested from Edie's own body. Unfortunately, she developed staph infections and gangrene, requiring more surgery. But she did keep her leg.

The recovery took several years and left Edie with a functioning left leg, albeit two inches shorter than her right leg and grossly disfigured with a series of scars, protrusions, contusions and small holes or crevices up and down the limb that people fixated on when they first met her, and even after they knew her well.

During her long stay in the hospital she had few visitors other than Candy Stripers and volunteers from the local Catholic Church. Her husband David went back to work selling cars at a Cadillac dealership in Seneca Falls, New York, and presumably was working too many hours, including weekends, to make the trip to Ashland with any regularity. Edie's father, Sal Donato, was spending most of his time now in New York City, dining and drinking at fine establishments and hobnobbing with the likes of lawyers, doctors and, it was believed, certain figures of the Italian underworld, some of whom, on occasion, would accompany him to Geneva and eat in the private "Mercato Room" in Morelli's Restaurant, where Lessa would cook for them and generally wait on them as though they were royalty. Days after Vicki was born in March 1956 in the Ashland hospital where Edie was being treated, it was decided by someone, it was never sure whom, that she would be taken to stay with Dennis and Nick in Geneva. They were living at Morelli's since their father worked into the evenings and did not arrive home until after their bedtime. Lessa was their de facto parent; her energy was boundless. For reasons unknown, David's family rarely visited Edie during her lengthy hospitalization, even though the distance between Ashland

and Dublin was less than a hundred miles. They could have been busy with work, as well.

Edie was sick, aggrieved and alone in Ashland for months, and she would come to speak of that period with equal parts indignation and forgiveness. The young surgeon Siklosi left for brighter prospects at a hospital in the Midwest that specialized in orthopedics and neurosurgery, and after that Edie's condition, like her spirit, ceased to improve and instead took a turn for the worse. She would speak fondly of Dr. Siklosi in later years, recollecting his boyishly round face, rosy cheeks and blonde fuzzy whiskers that reminded her of a freshly picked peach from the Red Jacket Orchard & Farm stand on Route 14 in Geneva. So she nicknamed him "Peaches," which he did not seem to mind. Mostly she spoke of his bedside manner and tender charm that always made her feel like she was his favorite patient, even his only patient.

Edie's general health beyond her mangled leg was deteriorating almost daily by the summer of 1956. She developed severe stomach ulcers and her nerves kept her awake most nights despite medication. She worried about Dennis because by the time he came out of a coma three days after the accident, she was sedated most of the time and was not able to hold and comfort him before he was taken back to Geneva. David regained consciousness sooner than Dennis and wept, probably for the first and last time in his adulthood, when he whispered to his wife that Dennis was awake and aware and that doctors predicted a complete recovery. While the newspaper accounts of the accident reported that Nick was "bruised," he did not suffer a single day in his life nor bear a single scar anywhere on his body related to the crash. Not physically or visibly. Still, Edie did not know for herself the exact condition of her two young sons. Even regular and upbeat phone updates from her mother and sister, Lucky, did not convince Edie of the well-being of her boys.

It is not clear to this day whether the circumstances of Edie's diminishing health involved neglect or incompetence or both. But it was unquestionably true to her, at least, that the hospital care was indifferent at best. Most days she remained in bed lying on her back with her left leg hoisted at a forty-five-degree angle in a pulley of sorts, and was not assisted out of her bed for routine exercise or even rolled to one side or the other for a change of position. Trips to the bathroom were the only exception. While she was pregnant with Vicki, doctors told her it was best not to move too much or lay on her sides. Once every couple of days she would be helped up and allowed to stand on her one good leg and stretch her bones for a few minutes. She developed bed sores and was told by the staff that they were a normal part of the healing process. Edie went several days at a time without being bathed; her leg beneath the cast would itch insatiably despite her attempts to scratch with a straightened metal clothes hanger that one of the Candy Stripers helped her devise. Without hesitation or any apparent conscience, the staff doctors prescribed morphine virtually around the clock for all her symptoms and discomforts, and probably through only the good grace of God was she spared a lifelong addiction, as was Vicki, who spent seven months in her mother's belly following the accident. But in the mid-1950s there was little recourse - medical, legal or otherwise - and even if there was it would have been a charge the weakened Edie could not have pursued on her own. Surely it was her strong will and determination to reunite with and care for her family back in the cradle of her beloved Geneva that kept her from going mad, and conceivably even from surrendering altogether to her pain and suffering, an option that at times she thought the lesser of all evils.

On February 9, 1956, Edie's twenty-seventh birthday, her mother –
Lessa – walked through the door of the room her daughter shared
with a woman named Ruth Cloesmeyer, a patient being treated for a
kidney disorder. David had been Lessa's only visitor up to that point.
Lessa took the Greyhound Bus from Geneva to Cleveland and then a
$35 cab ride from Cleveland to Ashland, about sixty-five miles, with
a change of clothes and a bag of homemade meatballs and a loaf of
Italian bread in the same large suitcase that her parents might very
well have packed when they came to America from Italy nearly five
decades earlier.

The moment Edie saw her mother she burst into tears. So did
Lessa, which was expected. What was not expected was that Mrs.
Cloesmeyer, who was younger than Lessa but older than Edie, would
also sob noticeably. She barely knew her roommate and never met
Lessa, yet somehow she sensed the crux of the reunion. Mother and
daughter embraced for several minutes as Mrs. Cloesmeyer cried
even more loudly.

"Why is she crying?" Lessa asked, curiously, as she eased back from
Edie's embrace.

"I don't know Ma."

"Who are you?" Lessa asked the woman.

"I'm Ruth Cloesmeyer."

"Oh. You want a meatball?"

Lessa sat in a nondescript visitor's chair beside Edie's bed and they
talked for several hours about Dennis and Nick. Dennis was doing
fine and Dr. Dooley, their Geneva pediatrician until, it seems, the
boys had more hair on their balls than he had on his head, said

he was completely recovered from the concussion he received in the car accident. No one in the family was ever totally convinced of that. It could be that Dennis was born dim witted, but most believed his brain was scrambled when his head smashed into the dashboard of the Packard. That's not to say his brain stopped working altogether, just the parts responsible for rational thinking and physical coordination.

Nick was doing fine as well, in Dr. Dooley's medical opinion. But Lessa didn't need a doctor to tell whether her grandkids were healthy or sickly. She could feel their foreheads and make her own diagnosis. She told Edie that Nicky had "head" problems. "He's not sick, Edie. He's a ball breaker. He don't sleep at night, and during the day he sleeps like he's dead. He won't eat his baby food. He likes fried baloney and macaroni with oil and garlic."

"Ma, how the frig did you figure he likes fried baloney? Did he ask for it? He doesn't even have teeth." Edie was eight months pregnant with Vicki, her leg inside the cast was fizzing, and the meatballs had given her heartburn. She was percolating inside and out.

"It was on the table one night and he grabbed some with his hand and put it in his mouth. Even the hot pepper," Lessa said. "Right from his highchair."

"Jesus Christ Ma," Edie scolded, doing her best now to prop herself up in the bed. "Do ya think the fried baloney and hot peppers might be why he ain't sleeping at night?"

"No Edie. Swear to God. He eats it in the morning too and he sleeps all afternoon."

"For Christ's sake. Can you just give him his bottle at night?"

"He don't take a bottle no more. He likes to drink with a straw."

"Does he eat meatballs too?" Ruth asked, wiping cold tomato sauce from her lips.

"Yeah. We gotta mash them up for him. Dennis likes to bite into them whole. I put one on a fork and tell him it's a meatball lollipop. Oh, how he laughs."

As the night went on Lessa explained to Edie how only certain people could hold Nicky. For example, Christian, Lessa's godson, could hold him, feed him, and put him down for a nap without resistance. On the other hand, his Uncle Gus only had to look at him and he would hiss like a scared kitten. Marco, with his mutilated left forefinger, was not even allowed to be in the same room as Nick. After a while everybody that passed through the back room at Morelli's knew who could and who could not handle the boy.

There was a break in the conversation that seemed much longer than it was. Lessa stared at the cast on her daughter's leg. Her eyes teared again.

"What happened Edie?" Lessa's tone was not of anger, more palpable disgust.

"What do you mean?"

"The accident? Did he fall asleep at the wheel? Your husband?"

"I don't know Ma." Her tone also had a tinge of disgust. And sadness.

"Was you sleeping? Your husband don't tell us nothing."

"I don't know. Maybe. Maybe we was all sleeping. I remember putting my leg up on the dashboard to stretch. Dennis was sleeping with his head in my lap. That's all I remember."

"I told you to make him stop if he got tired."

"Jesus Christ Ma. I don't want to talk about this."

Lessa pulled a leather photo album out of her giant suitcase and set it on the edge of the bed. It was the photo album from Edie's wedding, a source of great pride for Lessa. The restaurant was doing well, and the family was making a name for itself in Geneva. The people who lived on the other side of town, the furthest from the railroad tracks, would come to Morelli's for dinner and some would duck into the kitchen from the dining room through the swinging aluminum doors to compliment Lessa on her food; pay their respects. Morelli's meatballs were becoming famous beyond Geneva into the surrounding towns of the Finger Lakes, as far away as Penn Yan. The meatballs were made with three kinds of meat – beef chuck, pork shoulder and ground veal – with a handful of freshly grated parmesan cheese, several cloves of finely chopped garlic and lots of fresh parsley that Lessa grew in the garden behind the restaurant. It was an ambrosial combination of ingredients. The recipe included eggs and a small amount of breadcrumbs, less breadcrumbs than meat, to be sure. But what really set Morelli's meatballs apart was that they were cooked slowly and entirely in Lessa's thick, dark tomato sauce. The other Italian restaurants in the area deep fried their meatballs in oil first and then let them cook through in tomato sauce, which not only made for a terribly inconsistent mouth feel – part crunchy, part mushy – but also left the sauce thin and oily. Lessa's meatballs were the perfect texture – consistently soft on the outside and the inside and soaked with sauce like little round sponges. Her sauce was always hearty, not oily.

It wasn't on the menu but for the men who came into the bar for a shot and a beer after working the late shift at the United Can factory across the tracks from Morelli's, Lessa mashed the soft, sauce-soaked meatballs on top of a thick slice of fresh Italian bread from Delano's bakery, then covered it with a long hot pepper, topped it with a second piece of bread and covered the sandwich with a ladle of tomato sauce. Sprinkled with parmesan to taste.

With the restaurant doing so well Lessa decided to throw Edie – her oldest child and first to be married – a grand wedding with a mass at Saint Thomas Aquinas Church on Exchange Street and a reception at Morelli's. Like everything Lessa did, it would be a family affair. Even the church was flanked by buildings with huge signs bearing the family name: Donato Painters, Donato Pizza, Big D Lighting. Presiding over the nuptials was Reverend John Donato, a cousin.

The wedding was on Saturday April 18, 1952, a picture-perfect spring day, and Edie was a picture-perfect bride. She wore a spring gown with a lace edge and neckline, and a delicate Chantilly lace and satin veil. Sparkling beads and sequins accented her entire ensemble. She carried a bouquet of camellias, lilies of the valley and satin streamers with violets. The Maid of Honor was Edie's sister, Roseanne "Lucky" Donato.

Lessa had it exactly right.

As they thumbed through the pages of photographs, mother and daughter began to cry. They did not speak a word but they both thought that Edie might never be as happy as she was on that day in April 1953. She might never stride as naturally or smile as brightly. Her sleep would be rough and uneven, and sometimes she would feel the same insatiable itch on her left leg that she felt in the hospital, even though the cast would be long gone. Life would never be the same for either one of them. The accident broke one leg, and two hearts.

CHAPTER NINE
Back with the Boys

The earliest memories Dennis and Nick had of their mother were of her hobbling uncomfortably in a hard cast covering her left leg from her thigh all the way down to her toes. They were living in a two-story house on North Walnut Street and Edie spent most nights sleeping on the sofa in the living room on the first floor because she could not easily climb the stairs to her bedroom. The brothers must have been four and six years old; possibly five and seven. Neither felt sad about their mother's leg being in a cast, and they certainly did not remember how it came to be. It was the only way they knew her. To them it was normal. But they did know that she laid on the sofa at night crying right up until they fell asleep. By now their father had taken a job managing an auto plant in Buffalo, New York, about ninety miles from Geneva, and was spending as many nights there as he was at home.

"Why is she crying?" Nick would ask his older brother.

"Because she's watching a sad movie on the TV," Dennis would answer. "And because she knows you're an idiot. Go to sleep."

Dennis and Nick came down to breakfast one morning and their mother's cast and crutches were gone. She was using a cane to get around. The boys had the run of the house. They weren't bad kids, at least not in a malevolent way. But they made no concessions to their mother's disability, or her inability. They learned early where they could build forts and castles out of pillows and blankets and make booby traps that would challenge even an able-bodied marauder. They were mischievous, but by no means extraordinary. They knew what they could and could not get away with, and where to hide when they stretched the boundaries. Mostly they knew to stay out of reach of their mother's cane, especially the end that could hook and pull them in. If they could do that they would stay out of harm's way, despite their transgressions.

The two brothers spent most days in their backyard, a small rectangular patch of uneven land that was mostly hardened dirt, overgrown bushes, and a clump of small trees at the part of the yard furthest from the house. Whatever trouble they created back there stayed there, and if their mother found out, she either didn't care or couldn't do anything about it anyway. It was a sanctuary. At some point their father made a patio with cement tiles, but over a short period of time the rain and mud and general topography separated the tiles, causing most of them to crack. He put up a lattice partition to separate the patio from the driveway and he attempted to grow some type of vines up the wooden structure. To David Poole this was landscape design. To Dennis and his brother, it was a giant wall that they needed to scale in order to invade an enemy fort.

The best time to play in the backyard was right after a mid-summer rain. The small trees and weeds released a sweet scent into the cool, damp air. The yellow dandelion flowers glowed, and if the boys threw them hard enough against the side of their white house, they would splat like paint caps. The dirt hardpan became a muddy slip-and-slide. Once, after such an August rain, they tracked mud through the back door and into the kitchen to filch slices of thick-cut bologna from the Frigidaire.

"With those filthy hands?" Edie screamed, scaring the boys senseless as she stood in the doorway between the dining room and kitchen, waiving her cane. She had Vicki close in tow as always. Vicki was like an appendage attached to her mother's right leg - her good leg. "With those filthy hands you're taking *my* food out of *my* refrigerator. I just mopped *my* goddamn floor!" Edie took official ownership of everything in the house. It was always "my house," "my kitchen," "my floor," "my food," "my god."

She demanded that Dennis and Nick clean the kitchen floor "til it fricken' shines" or they'd get no dinner and no snack after their baths. No snack? That was preposterous. No cupcakes? No peanut butter on crackers? No popcorn? No ice cream? No milk and cookies? She had subjected them to this cruel comeuppance on other occasions, most recently when they replaced four Morelli's meatballs with four of their own homemade mud balls in a pot of tomato sauce Edie had simmering on the stove. Like her mother, she always let her sauce simmer, sometimes for half a day. That way the sauce would be thick and rich, and the meat would cook slowly and be soft and moist, not tough and dried out. After the first hour or so the entire house smelled like the Morelli's kitchen. When the back door was open the neighbors could smell the stewing sauce from their yards. The brothers Poole might have gotten away with their mud balls had Vicki not made her "yucky" face when Dennis spoon fed her a few small pieces. "Why you little bastards!" Edie screamed.

If she followed through on her threat over the muddy kitchen floor, Dennis and Nick would lie in their beds dying of starvation with skin sagging from their bones, screaming at the top of their lungs. Begging for a morsel, a crumb. Their stomachs would grumble so loudly the people next door would complain and dogs would howl up and down North Walnut Street. Dennis would threaten to call the police and have his hag of a mother arrested for torture. Nick would promise to run away and find a mother who really loved him.

They knew they had only a short while to get the kitchen floor squeaky clean and sparkling or suffer their mother's merciless wrath. They couldn't tell time to the minute but had a decent sense of it. For instance, they knew that Vicki had just been fed and that it was time for her bath. Then she would get tucked in with a story. Vicki would never let her mother leave the room until the story was over, and that was the only thing Dennis and Nick could not anticipate because they didn't know which story, or stories, their mother would read to Vicki that night. It was always Vicki who decided on the particulars, and it would depend on how tired she was. Sometimes the reading would be long, six to ten pages, and sometimes short, one to three pages. The difference between the longer stories and shorter ones could be as much as the big hand on the clock moving by seven or eight numbers.

All the stories came from a book called "365 Bedtime Stories" written by Nan Gilbert and illustrated by Jill Elgin, although throughout the years there were discussions, among whom it is not known, that the author's name was a pseudonym. "365 Bedtime Stories" was published in 1955 and Lucky gave it to her sister Edie the week Nick was born. Edie must not have done much reading to Nick before the accident because it was just now starting to show some wear on the pages. Vicki was by far the biggest beneficiary of Aunt Lucky's gift.

The 365 different stories all took place on "What A Jolly Street," and there was a subtle continuity among all the families that lived there. It was a cul-de-sac with its own school, store, farm, and a pond. Edie would say to Vicki, "See, it's just like our family. All your aunts and uncles and cousins come and go as they please. We're all just one big family."

Dennis and Nick managed to clean up all the mud using six rolls of toilet paper and a couple pairs of their mom's underwear they picked off the clothesline, but they were left with a dull looking floor, definitely not up to Edie's idea of "fricken' shines." Nick ran upstairs to listen outside of Vicki's bedroom door and reported back to his brother that their mother was still waiting for Vicki to select that night's story. Dennis figured they had until the big hand of the clock that hung on the wall over the stove made it all the way to the six. That would make it a familiar time to him, usually the time when Edie limped down the stairs to start their dinner.

"How does Mom make the floor so shiny?" Nick asked.

"She uses wax," Dennis said. "She always tells us to stay out of the kitchen whenever she waxes the floor, right?"

"So, where's the wax?"

They went from cupboard to cupboard to find wax, and since Dennis was just learning to read, they opened every can, canister and container hoping to identify any substance that looked like wax. They finally came upon a big blue can with fancy red letters that Dennis proudly sounded out into a word – C-R-I-S-C-O. "I think this is the floor stuff Mom uses," Dennis said. "I hear her say this word a lot to herself when she's in the kitchen." He stuck his fingers in the can and best he could tell the thick, slippery white stuff was exactly what they were looking for.

"Yeah, this is it. It smells like wax," Dennis said. "I smell it all the time when Mom's in the kitchen."

There were two more rolls of toilet paper in the bathroom closet, so Nick grabbed them, and the boys went to work waxing the kitchen floor with the Crisco. It was like magic. It went on quickly and easily and it made the floor sparkle like a new dime. They were having fun. No wonder their mother waxed the floor so often. It must have brought her a great deal of enjoyment. And no wonder she kept so much toilet paper in the house.

They did such a good job they were certain to get a special bedtime snack on this night. Perhaps their mom's famous Apple Brown Betty, or a Banana Cream Pie. Possibly a hot fudge sundae with whipped cream and peanuts. They could hear their mother coming down the stairs at her familiar uneven pace. Good leg. Bad leg. Good leg. Bad leg. They waited anxiously at the end of the kitchen furthest from the door she would be walking through. They were smiling widely. She was fixed on their beaming faces and never even looked down at the glistening kitchen floor.

Then things went bad. Out of the corner of her eye Edie noticed the wads of soiled toilet paper – eight rolls in all – spilling out of the sink, and on the counter adjacent to the sink an opened can of Crisco and some shriveled underpants that looked oddly familiar to her. Before she could make the connection, Edie stepped onto the kitchen floor and instantly both feet flew up into the air and she landed ass-first. Nick was sure he saw her rear end bounce off the floor and land for a second time, even harder. She tried fiercely – and fruitlessly – to get to her feet by rolling over and using her hands and knees, but the more she tried the more she flailed away and the faster she wound up flat on her face. Dennis could see the rage in her eyes. She was too angry to speak and the boys were too scared to move. She kept trying to stand up and kept sliding back down. On one attempt she reached out to grab Nick – the closest to her – but he stretched back far enough to avoid her deadly grasp. That's when Dennis and Nick knew for sure they had to get out of the kitchen or get hurt badly, never mind being denied their delicious bedtime snacks. But the floor was just as slippery for the boys as it was for their crippled mother. There they were, the three of them – mother crawling on all fours to get to the sons, and the sons climbing over each other to escape out the back door into the safety of the yard. While Edie had vengeful determination on her side, Dennis and Nick had the benefit of youth and four working legs. They managed to get into the yard just as their mom was using the kitchen table to prop herself upright. She stumbled to the back door by anchoring against anything stable along the way, and yelled through the screen, "Get your asses in here and wait for me to come out of the bathroom!" The youngsters were chin-scratching their next move when they heard their mother scream again, this time from the bathroom window and even more frantically: "Where the fuck is all the toilet paper?"

CHAPTER TEN

Out at Home

Not long after the "Crisco Incident," as it became known, Edie decided it was time to go back to work. The family could use the money and she figured it would be safer than tending to Dennis and Nick, and easier than humping Vicki around on her hip all day. Edie got her old job back at LoMoro's Butcher Shop on the Old Waterloo Road, about eight miles outside of Geneva. Mr. LoMoro, who looked and smelled like a rib roast, met Edie several years earlier in the back room at Morelli's while she was rolling meatballs for the restaurant and he was delivering fresh pork shoulder.

"You know what the secret ingredient is in those meatballs?" he asked back then.

LET THE SAUCE SIMMER

"If I did it wouldn't be a secret," Edie cracked. "I guess you better not tell me. I could lose my job."

"I'm glad you warned me," Mr. LoMoro said, smiling.

Mr. LoMoro must have liked Edie's chutzpah because a few weeks later he asked Lessa if he could offer her a part time job "in the shop." If she could roll meatballs, he thought, she already had a leg up on most of his other part-timers. Edie was out of high school by a couple of years at the time and had just started dating David Poole, and Lessa sensed they were getting too serious. She wasn't that crazy about him, either. She thought he was arrogant; in general had an air about him that came across as being too good for the family. If Edie took the job in Waterloo it would be less time they could spend together. David would move on, Lessa figured.

Edie won over Mr. LoMoro quickly and completely. She had a maturity beyond her years to the extent that Mr. LoMoro let her drive the store van to make deliveries, even though she had her driver's license for merely two weeks. Soon after that she was behind the counter taking orders and cutting meat – nothing too intricate, mostly just trimming and tying the beef tenderloins. She liked it but missed driving the van. Edie always had a propensity for the culinary arts, a gift that would become evident years later when she took over behind the stove at Morelli's.

Meanwhile, Lessa's plan failed. Edie worked at LoMoro's Butcher Shop right up until Dennis was born – Dennis Anthony Poole, son of David Dennis Poole. Grandson of Eric Poole, of the Dublin, Ohio Pooles.

With their mother back at work and their father taking jobs further from home, Dennis, Nick, and Vicki spent most of the daylight hours at 59 Lehigh Lane. Their Grandma Lessa was once again their primary authority, although throughout the day there were plenty of people coming and going in the back room at Morelli's who took it upon themselves to watch over the three Poole children. Workers at Morelli's didn't have job descriptions as such, and even if they did, "taking care of the Poole kids" would not have been included. But everyone affiliated with Morelli's, whether they were family, knew of Edie's situation and probably felt a moral obligation to pitch in. These people, during the normal course of their workdays, had various responsibilities, like cleaning the house, making macaroni and ravioli, baking pies, rolling meatballs, organizing the walk-in refrigerator, washing dishes, and doing the laundry. It was a big house to care for and the restaurant and bar also required daily maintenance – floors waxed, glasses washed, ice carried up in buckets from the basement to the wells behind the bar, fruit cut.

Somehow, between all those chores, the Poole kids were never out of reach of a pinch on the cheek or a swat on the ass, depending on the circumstances. Every Morelli's worker was authorized and obliged to administer either while managing their assigned duties.

As kids, they didn't think about living in a normal house like all their friends; a home where the father worked and the mother didn't and they met at the front door every night at around half past five. The children in these families would be done with their homework or their chores, greeted dad and then they all sat down to a hot meal followed by vanilla ice cream. But Dennis and his brother could not imagine a better place than 59 Lehigh Lane to squander their youth. It was like living in a castle with adventures waiting down every hallway and behind every closed door. Outside there was a gravel parking lot as big as Yankee Stadium that didn't get crowded with cars until the restaurant was busy later in the evening. It was a wonderful space for whiffle ball and tag, for riding bikes. There were enough bushes and trees around the perimeter to play hide-and-seek and there was a garden in the far corner of the lot that had a tree with red, juicy cherries and sturdy branches low enough to the ground that made it easy to climb once they poached all the low-hanging fruit. A few times a season they would get chased from the garden by an adult, but that was just another game to them.

Despite the great outdoors, their best times were wandering around the cavernous house. Every day they found something new to explore – a room, a closet, a chest of drawers stuffed with bric-a-brac and important-looking papers. Once, Nick found a pocketknife and immediately carved his initials on top of a desk. He got his ass kicked by three different aunts and a man who may or may not have been an uncle.

CHAPTER ELEVEN
The Early Years

David Poole began spending even more time away from home once his wife came out of her cast. Most of Edie's free time was spent with Vicki, the baby. Dennis and Nick were fortunate to have older cousins like Franky, Vinny and Michael to help them navigate the flux of their youth. The older boys smoked cigarettes, drank beer, cursed, drove cool cars, chased girls, and talked back to their parents. They were everything the young brothers wanted to be, and they looked up to their cousins as role models.

On the other hand, Dennis and Nick – Edie's sons and the oldest of Lessa's eleven grandchildren – were by no means role models to anybody. By rite of passage, and stature, Dennis and Nick should have been assigned some management responsibilities for the smaller kids, but generally they were not even trusted to feed the stray cats. The last time they were ever asked to look after one of their younger cousins – a tea kettle-shaped kid named Charlie whom everyone called Cheech – they thought it a good idea to take him on a tour of the expansive upstairs, a labyrinth of rooms, closets and chambers above the bar and restaurant. Some of the rooms were completely sequestered, others were adjoining. Some rooms had windows with views only into other rooms without a glimpse of daylight or starry nights; time stood still in these rooms. All the rooms had a standard issue crucifix hanging on the wall directly opposite the door – it was the first thing you saw when you came into the room – and thick, dark, full-length drapes. The rooms smelled like Lemon Pledge and mothballs.

Dennis showed his pudgy cousin a storage cubby in the sitting area upstairs and told him it was where their Grandma Lessa kept all the Christmas candy. The cubby holes in Morelli's were crawl spaces with only one way in and out and no electricity. Now, in Dennis's defense, his cousin could have already shit in his pants before he was locked in the dark cubby hole, not after, even though it was not until he was crawling out that Nick noticed the overpowering stench coming from Cheech's floppy trousers. He had been known to crap in his pants on much less traumatic occasions. And to be fair, while he was only four years old, he was big for his age. Dennis thought he overreacted to the whole thing, just as he believed at the time that the punishment was much too severe. First, his Grandma Lessa wound up and smacked Dennis with a giant steel soup ladle directly in the back of his neck. There was so much torque in her swing that it left a welt on his skin the exact circumference of the rounded ladle. By the time she got to Nick she was a little winded and could only muster half a swing, but she caught him square on his right forearm with a blow hard enough to jingle the coins in his pocket.

The brothers were standing in their familiar "time-out" corners in the parlor on the first floor of Morelli's, licking their wounds, when their mother returned from LoMoro's and got the full version from a few different bystanders. What happened next was, to them, almost as bad as the beating they got from their grandmother, though Edie never laid a hand on them.

"I'm disgusted with you two," she said, decidedly more tired than angry. "He's just a little boy, and you were supposed to watch him, not scare the shit out of him."

In his bones Nick could feel her disappointment, and he tried to reassure her, in earnest. "But Ma, we think he shit in his pants before we scared it out of him." It wasn't the best case to build.

"Oh yeah?" Edie said. "Now you're gonna stand in these goddamn corners until you shit in your own pants!"

Even when they were minding their own business, trouble seemed to find Dennis and Nick. Once, on a rainy Saturday afternoon, they were playing with a set of walkie-talkies Edie bought for them at the five-and-dime store on Castle Street. Dennis was upstairs and Nick was in the living room on the first floor until he got chased out by his Uncle Gus, who was taking a nap. "Why don't you go play outside like a normal kid," he snarled.

"It's raining," Nick said.

"Raining my ass," Gus snapped back. He always repeated things that were said to him with "my ass" attached to the end of his response.

"It's cold outside, Uncle Gus."

"Cold my ass."

"I'm hungry, Uncle Gus."

"Hungry my ass."

"My mother wants to talk to you about your language, Uncle Gus."

"Your mother my ass."

"Uncle Gus, my mom says you're a pain in her ass."

"Her ass my ass."

Nick told Dennis on the walkie-talkie that he was coming upstairs. *"Over,"* he squawked into the radio. At the top of the stairs Nick ducked into the first bedroom with an open door. It belonged to their teenage cousins, Vinny and Michael.

It was the biggest bedroom in Morelli's and by far the coolest. Vinny and Michael had their own beds, dressers and desks, and a lot of space in between. Dennis and Nick shared a bedroom in their house on North Walnut Street, and while they had separate beds, they shared a dresser and a nightstand; there was no room for even a single desk. They had one lamp on top of the nightstand between their beds, and they always fought over when it should be turned off for the night. Vinny and Michael had reading lamps on each desk, a very colorful lava lamp on a table in the corner, and even a black light that made teeth glow in the dark. Most noticeably though, on every wall in their bedroom hung at least one poster of a beautiful girl wearing a very skimpy bathing suit. Nick may not have had much interest in real girls at that point in his life, but he couldn't help gazing up at these paper replicas wearing hardly any clothes whenever he walked into the room. Vinny told him these were all the girls that he and Michael had dated, or were dating. A few years later Nick would come to know their names – Raquel Welch, Joey

Heatherton, Ann Margret, Claudia Cardenale, Elke Sommer, Julie Newmar.

On this rainy Saturday Nick was standing in the middle of the bedroom rotating his glance from one stunning set of bulging breasts to the next, completely oblivious to Dennis's chatter over the walkie-talkie. *"Come in Nicky. Come in. It's Dennis. Where are you? Come in."* What did get Nick's attention, however, was the sound of the front door opening and closing at the bottom of the stairs, just below the bedroom. He heard footsteps coming closer and a girl's giggle. At first, he thought it was one of his younger cousins looking for him and Dennis, probably for dinner, so he hid under a bed with the plan to roll out and startle her. Then he heard his cousin Michael call out, "What are you doing up here?" He was talking to Dennis who was standing suspiciously at the other end of the hall. Dennis, too scared to be coherent, muttered something benign.

"Go downstairs. Your mother's probably looking for you," Michael yelled.

Immediately the bedroom door closed, and Nick was under the same bed that Michael and the giggling girl fell on to. A squeaking noise came faintly through his walkie-talkie and he knew it was Dennis trying to warn him. He fumbled blindly for the on/off button but only managed to increase the volume. The only other way he could think of to silence his walkie-talkie was to hold down the "talk" button so that Dennis could hear him, but he could not hear Dennis. Pieces of clothing began dropping on the floor all around Nick. A belt, pants, a shirt, a bra, another shirt, a sock, another sock.

Nick didn't move a muscle; he took short breaths. He could feel his sweating thumb sliding off the "talk" button on the side of the walkie-talkie. Still, he thought he could make it until it was time for the girl to go home or someone called Michael for dinner. He would be the only one to ever know about Michael's carnal conquest.

All Nick could hear now was breathing and moaning. This could not go on much longer. It didn't sound like either one of them was having fun. He heard the girl say, "We should stop. What if someone comes in?"

"No one will come in," Michael assured. "Everybody's downstairs. They're probably eating."

"I know, but I shouldn't be here," she whimpered. "It's just not me."

"Don't worry," Michael said. "Whoever you are you're exactly where you should be."

As it turned out, yes, everybody else was downstairs. They were eating. But they were also listening to everything going on in the bedroom through Dennis's walkie-talkie that was resting on the middle of the table as he dug into a plate of spaghetti and meatballs. Sofia and Gus were sitting at the table in a total stupor. Christian was there, belly laughing. Buster was at the table with his new wife, her face as red as the sauce-covered meatballs. Two or three of Dennis's younger cousins and his little sister Vicki were there, though they had no idea what the conversation coming from the walkie-talkie was about. And, of course, Edie was in the room, wondering what Dennis and Nick could possibly have to do with this, and knowing, for certain, that it had to be something.

"Turn that goddamn thing off," Gus yelled.

Dennis kept eating, completely indifferent to the fuss around him.

Gus grabbed the walkie-talkie and fumbled with it before turning it off. "Where the hell is the other one?" he shouted.

"Nicky has it. I think he's in Michael's room," Dennis said calmly, strands of spaghetti hanging from his lower lip.

At the same exact moment, no less than five people sitting around the table yelped: "Nicky?" At the same exact next moment, the same five people got up from the kitchen table, ran down the hall and up the stairs to Michael's room. Gus got there first and threw open the door.

"What are you doing?" Michael yelled. "Get out of my room!"

Suddenly, Nick saw a hand - he knew it was a girl's hand because it was sleek and smooth and had painted fingernails - reach down from the bed and pick up some of the clothes. First the bra. Then underpants and a shirt with a single swipe. Out of shear embarrassment, the girl rolled herself off the side of the bed opposite the door and temporarily out of view of the stunned and gawking audience that had just burst onto the scene. As she hit the floor her bare-naked ass bounced a mere inch or two away from Nick's face. He hadn't seen many asses in his life up to that point, but figured instantly that as asses go, this must have been one of God's finest. Curiously, he poked his right forefinger into one of the perfectly formed butt cheeks, much the same way he would poke a ball of Morelli's pizza dough just to see what it felt like. Before the slight indentation in the girl's fleshy rump popped back into place, Nick heard his mother call out: "Where's Nicky?" On her gimpy leg, she was the last to reach the bedroom.

"Why would Nicky be in here?" Michael screamed. "Why would any of you people be in here?"

"Because he has the other walkie-talkie!" Edie yelled back.

"Other walkie-talkie? What the fuck are you talking about?"

Just when Nick was about to be yanked from under the bed and likely have his ass jacked by a range of adults, Vinny walked into the room. He had not been sitting at the table in the back room with the others listening to Dennis's walkie-talkie, so he was unaware, but not unamused. That is until he noticed that the girl now standing beside the bed buttoning her blouse was the same girl he had been dating for the past three weeks.

Nick became no more than a bystander, although he still got a good ass whacking from his mother once the smoke cleared. Dennis got one too, which made Nick's whacking sting a little less. The more painful consequence was the rift between Vinny and Michael. It would take a while to get fixed, but like everything at 59 Lehigh Lane, it would most certainly get fixed. One way or another. But it would take more than just a lock on their bedroom door.

Vinny and Michael were about four years apart in age, but the moral maturity gap was wider than that. Vinny was born in 1944, the second son of Sofia and Geno Riotto. Ronnie Riotto was born a year and sixteen days earlier, and soon after was diagnosed with polio, which would claim his life near his twelfth birthday. During those twelve short years the two boys developed a unique kinship that certainly shaped Vinny's lifelong nature and character as a nurturing, compassionate individual. From the time he started grade school, Vinny assumed a big brother role to his older sibling. Because of his physical limitations, which became more significant as the months and years passed, Ronnie required constant assistance to perform routine tasks, like getting dressed, going to the bathroom, and navigating a spoonful of food from his plate to his mouth. It was Vinny who answered the call virtually around the clock while their parents kept busy working in the restaurant. By the time Michael came along in 1948 Vinny was fully vested in Ronnie's care and afforded little attention to the youngest of the three brothers. Michael did just fine on his own, even after his father left the family, and in fact developed a confident and independent persona that he would carry throughout adulthood, sometimes to a fault. He took more risks. He sought less guidance and direction. He was opinionated and unshakable. He disdained authority anywhere it existed.

If you crossed Michael, you probably wound up in a fist fight or could have suffered his malice in more subtle ways. He was the quarterback on the high school football team. In the summer before his senior season a teammate tried to birddog his girlfriend, who, by the way, used to be Vinny's girlfriend. The friend never got the date, and in fact went the following season without getting a single catchable pass from Michael. It didn't make any difference that in the previous season the friend was Michael's favorite pass catcher, and to this day holds the single season pass-catching record for the school. Nor did it matter that the team might have forged a winning record had Michael not been so vindictive. The receiver thought he had locked up a college football scholarship until his disastrous senior year on the high school grid iron.

Now, had Vinny been the quarterback, and found himself with the same sense of betrayal, he probably would have thrown the ball to his nemesis anyway, for the good of the team. Of course, Vinny would never have been the quarterback, and his girlfriend would have more than likely gone out with her pursuer.

Only twice in Nick's recollection did he see even a flicker in Vinny's temper. The first time was when he caught Michael dabbling with his girlfriend during the walkie-talkie episode. The second incident happened when Nick was fourteen years old. He was in the rectory of Saint Thomas Aquinas church on Exchange Street with a few of his fellow Altar Boys. It was July 20, 1969 and Father James "Jimmy" O'Gara, who was officially or unofficially the overseer of Altar Boys at Saint Thomas Aquinas, had invited them all to the rectory to watch the first man ever walk on the moon. At the time Nick didn't really appreciate the significance of this historic milestone; the more important event to him was a party with some of his pals in a huge house with a million rooms, and somewhere, they were sure, many bottles of wine, the same sweet wine the Altar Boys secretly sipped before and after they served morning mass.

It was around eleven at night because Astronaut Neil Armstrong had just taken his famous "one small step" into the Sea of Tranquility at precisely 10:56PM Eastern Standard Time. While the rest of America was celebrating with champagne and other spirits, the only one in the rectory enjoying the sacred wine was Father Jimmy, and he was chasing it with his personal stash of sacred single malt scotch. He was a drinker. The parish officials knew it. The parishioners knew it. The blue hairs in the last few pews at 6AM weekday mass Monday through Friday knew it; they could smell it on his indigo chasuble as they took Holy Communion. This was a period when Catholic priests were revered; they were above social conventions and beyond reproach. They were holier-than-thou.

Father Jimmy was strangely close to his Altar Boys. He took them to secret swimming holes and let them skinny dip. He came to all their CYO (Catholic Youth Organization) basketball games and was always in the locker room to congratulate or console the boys as they emerged from the showers. On the night of July 20, 1969 at the Saint Thomas Aquinas rectory, a very intoxicated Father Jimmy commenced the first annual Altar Boy Wrestling Championship, even though their school did not have a wrestling team. He encouraged the wrestlers to strip down to their drawers so that they didn't tear their clothes.

That's about when Vinny came through the giant archway of the rectory library. He was delivering a stack of Morelli's pizzas Edie had promised the boys. Father Jimmy was slouched in a cushy chair with an empty rocks glass in one hand and a smoldering non-filter cigarette with a hanging ash in the other. He was wearing a soiled tee-shirt, yet his clerical collar was still relatively intact. Peter Marino had an unlit cigarette dangling from his lips and was clutching a near empty bottle of whiskey in the far corner of the room. Nick was lying flat on his back in his undies with Harold Durso sitting on his chest trying to press Nick's shoulders to the floor. In another corner of the room Colin Britt had wrapped himself in a blanket and was shivering, at least as far as Nick could tell looking backwards with Harold's nut sack inching closer to his chin. It took Vinny about three seconds to scan the entire room and make an assessment. In a fury he flung the pizza boxes to the side, shucked Harold from Nick's chest and grabbed the bottle of whiskey from Peter. He went to Colin, but Colin pushed him away. Everything happened so fast none of the boys knew what to make of the turn of events.

Vinny wasn't so angry at the Altar Boys, but furious with Father Jimmy. His temper ran too hot, too quickly for this to be his first consequential encounter with the cleric. Vinny bent at the waist until he was face to face with the drunk, slouching O'Gara. He grabbed him by his tee-shirt, taking more than a few strands of gray chest hair with it, and pulled him so close that the stench of booze and cigarettes gave his breath a visible tint. Vinny snarled something in Father Jimmy's right ear and then thrust him into his seat with a motion so violent his head snapped back, and he passed out. At the time Nick did not understand his older cousin's grievance with the priest nor with the boys' antics. He knew that just a few years earlier Vinny himself was an Altar Boy under Father Jimmy's watch, one of the reasons Nick decided to sign up himself, to follow in his cool cousin's footsteps. Why didn't Vinny appreciate the revelry? Why wasn't he with one of his gorgeous pin-up girlfriends so close to the stroke of midnight on New Year's Eve?

By Christmas Father James O'Gara was gone from the parish with little fanfare. The Monsignor announced during a Sunday mass that he had been reassigned. He was never heard from again. The church halted all types of activities for its Altar Boys beyond serving mass. The boys' locker room was declared off limits to anyone except for active and injured players, the coach, and the trainer. Colin Britt never came back to Saint Thomas Aquinas after the Christmas holidays; he enrolled in the public school on the other side of town because, the team was told, it was closer to his home and he wouldn't have to ride the bus every day. He was one of the better players on the basketball team and the other players would miss him, although they looked forward to playing against him in their annual cross-town rivalry game. But Colin never played school-boy basketball during the rest of his time in the Geneva school system.

Vinny never spoke of the incident again and Nick never asked. He did not mind that Vinny showed up that night, even though he ruined a perfectly good party and inaugural wrestling tournament.

On July 20, 1969, Neil Armstrong became the first man to walk on the moon. It was not what anybody in the rectory would remember most about that night.

Vinny's good nature killed him. He died on Friday, October 2, 1970 when the plane he was traveling on – one of two planes taking the

Wichita State University football team to Logan, Utah for a game against Utah State University – crashed into a mountain near the Continental Divide somewhere over Colorado. The plane that went down was carrying the starting players, head coach and athletic director, their wives, administrators, boosters, and family. The other plane had the reserve players, assistant coaches and other support staff. Vinny, a senior at Wichita State on the G.I. Bill, was the team's equipment manager and always traveled on the second plane. But three days earlier, on a Tuesday, just as he was gulping his last spoonful of tapioca in the main dining hall, a fire broke out in the kitchen. The rest of the students rushed toward the exits. Vinny ran into the kitchen and subdued the flames with a fire extinguisher that was hanging on a wall near the giant walk-in refrigerator. The only other person still in the fume-filled kitchen was Isaphine Harlan – her name badge said Issy so that's what the students called her. She was kneeling, facing the wall, coughing and gasping. The smoke was also getting to Vinny. He grabbed Issy by the fleshy part of her arm above the elbow and pulled her to her feet, no easy task considering this woman outweighed him by thirty pounds or more. He helped her wobble out of the kitchen, through a short corridor and into the fresh air. Fire trucks were pulling up and an ambulance was soon on the scene to take Issy to the infirmary. She was home a few hours later.

The next day **The Sunflower**, the campus newspaper, ran the story of the fire on the front page above the fold. Below the main headline, a smaller headline read: "Student braves blaze to rescue worker." After reading the story, which mentioned Vinny's role on the football team, Ben Wilson, the head football coach, personally invited Vinny to fly to Utah with him, side by side, on the first plane. It was the first time Vinny ever flew on the first plane.

CHAPTER TWELVE

The Back Room

If bricks and mortar could talk, 59 Lehigh Lane would, at varying times, curse you, comfort you, infuriate you, inspire you. It would tell you to go screw yourself, ask if you wanted something to eat or needed a place to sleep. It would offer you a few bucks for gas. Fifty-nine Lehigh Lane would repel aluminum siding, white lines on parking lots and fountain soda when you could have a crisp, cold 6.5-ounce bottle of pop. This old house would interrogate you about your friends, your weight, your acne and your prom date.

At 59 Lehigh Lane you could be in a room with ten other people and you might only know three or four by name. It didn't matter. You knew them and they knew you. Some rooms had thick carpets, some had tile on the floors, and some floors were wood – real wood, imperfect wood. There was a small closet at the end of the hallway between the front door and the eat-in kitchen that was crammed with tweed overcoats, moth-eaten sweaters, and brown and black fedoras. Against the back wall of the closet was a giant gray safe with a shiny silver dial in the center of a thick door.

There was at least one crucifix in every room, including the bathrooms.

The "back room" at 59 Lehigh Lane, just off the big kitchen, was like a tapestry of ill woven fabric that swirled in different directions without a discernable pattern. It was where the family took coffee, read the Racing Form, bet on horses, played cards and generally assembled and conversed whenever they weren't working in the kitchen, the restaurant, or the bar. There were the transients, the men and women who came and went without any reason to be there or, for that matter, any reason to leave. They weren't relatives, but they were family, at least that's how they were treated and how they represented. It's also the room where the family ate all its meals, except for Christmas Eve, the only night of the entire year other than Thanksgiving that the restaurant was closed. On Christmas Eve the extended family gathered in the restaurant dining room for an orgy of food and gifts. It was just family, but they crowded the place like it was open to the public and the food was free.

The back room was always filled with smoke. In the 1960s and seventies everybody smoked cigarettes, and anybody who didn't smoke didn't mind those who did. It wasn't an us-versus-them dynamic between smokers and non-smokers like it would become decades later. Gus smoked Pall Mall straights and was always picking tiny shards of tobacco from his lips. Sofia smoked whatever was in front of her without any preference because she never, ever, never inhaled. She probably blew more second-hand smoke into the back room than all the other smokers combined since none of her smoke was absorbed into her own lungs. She would take long pulls on her cigarette and instead of blowing the smoke out through puckered lips, like normal smokers, she just opened her mouth and let the smoke billow out in clouds so thick they hid her face. Christian smoked Marlboro because, to him, the brand reflected his own machismo. On Christmas every smoker would get a carton of their own brand from a Secret Santa, and they were genuinely grateful.

The only non-smoking regular in the back room was Dominic DiLorenzo, who smoked his last De Nobili Italian cigar the day he shot and killed Alberto Grillo in 1935 in the alleyway near Morelli's Restaurant. He did his twenty-one years in Attica and came back to Morelli's to live out his life. The children in the family, like Dennis and Nick and Cheech, weren't yet born when he went to prison, so they did not remember him getting out. He was always there. When he wasn't doing repairs around the house, he was sitting in the same corner of the back room closest to the window, or in the soft, drab easy chair in the living room just a couple of feet from the television. He stared at the television screen the same way he gazed out the window in the back room – expressionless, indifferent. Dominic didn't talk much to anyone but Lessa, and that was only in Italian or very choppy English that he must have picked up in prison. Sometimes it sounded like they were arguing. The only time Dominic paid any attention to anyone else would be when they spoke harshly to Lessa. He did not like that, and he let it be known by growling. Dominic and Lessa had a certain bond that made them close enough to look out for each other, and at the same time comfortable enough to bicker with one another. For whatever reason, Dominic also took to Edie. Whenever Lessa was too busy to bring him supper, Edie would fill in. Maybe that's why he was so fond of her. Maybe he felt sorry for her because of the accident.

Others brought Dominic his meals on occasion, but he remained unmindful of them.

If there was a soft side to Dominic it surfaced around the Christmas holidays. He used his pocketknife to separate walnuts perfectly at their seams, hollowed out the two halves, inserted a quarter stained with a dab of red nail polish and sealed the two halves back together with white Elmer's glue that was transparent when it dried. Then he would hand out the walnuts to all the kids, in no planned order, right up through Christmas night. The modified walnuts looked perfectly natural, so natural in fact that it could not be said what moved the youngsters to even open them in the first place. Walnuts weren't exactly at the top of an adolescent's Christmas list. The walnuts stuffed with painted coins became one of the family's favorite holiday traditions, right up there with Secret Santa and fried dough dipped in sugar.

As for the red polish, it was not pointless. The old jukebox in Morelli's bar was fussy; it would accept about half of the quarters in return for a selection and reject the other half through the change slot on the bottom of the machine, without any apparent logic. When customers asked the bartender to give them four quarters for a dollar bill, so they could feed the jukebox, invariably only two of the quarters yielded a song. That meant the jukebox would forfeit fifty percent of its potential revenue, or the customer would have to go back to the bar for more change. Either way it was a pain in the ass for someone. When he emptied the machine every week to put the change back into the bar's cash register, Dominic had the idea to dab each quarter he removed with a splash of red nail polish so that the bartender would only dole out quarters for the jukebox that had the best chance of producing music. As soon as the children learned the meaning of the color code, their Christmas quarters were deposited right back into the jukebox so that they could listen to their favorite holiday songs before the bar opened. Throughout his life Dennis cringed every time he heard "Christmas Don't Be Late" by Alvin and the Chipmunks.

Hypocrisy certainly had its place in the back room at Morelli's, especially when it came to religion. Despite all the holy crosses and bibles, the portraits of the Virgin Mary, the Rosary Beads and Saint Christopher medals, other than fearing the existence of hell no one much acknowledged the presence of God. Yet everyone fancied themselves devout Catholics because it was all they knew. Son of God was born on Christmas Day, died on the cross on Good Friday when he was a grown man – making all Fridays thereafter meatless for some reason – and rose from the grave on Easter Sunday. End of story.

The family had a Jewish friend named Sora Banka, the wife of a prominent local physician, who would visit Lessa and Sofia in the back room every couple of weeks. Once a year – in March or April – she would bring with her homemade Yiddish pastries called hamantashen, a three-cornered pocket cookie filled with prunes, nuts, dates, or the like. In Israel, hamantashen are called Oznei Haman, which translates literally to "Haman's Ears." The treat is typically associated with the Jewish holiday of Purim, and the cookie is a reference to Haman, the defeated villain in the Purim story. Mrs. Banka tried often to explain the symbolism to her two friends, but it always fell on deaf ears. Sofia and Lessa were quite fond of this woman and vice versa, and they typically had a pleasant visit even though they didn't have anything in common save for the fact that they were all born in Europe, wound up in Geneva, New York, and they did appreciate a good mid-week coffee klatch. Sofia and Lessa came to America from Italy with their parents and most of their belongings. They were not wealthy by any stretch, but they kept what was theirs. They spent their lives in Geneva and for the most part in the building at 59 Lehigh Lane. Sora Banka was smuggled out of Nazi-occupied Poland in 1943 by a sympathetic German businessman and arrived in America with only the clothes she was wearing. Her mother and father died in Litzmannstadt, the last ghetto in Poland to be emptied in August 1944. In America, Sora put herself through college and then taught European History at Hobart and William Smith Colleges in Geneva. She traveled the world, including several trips back to Poland to the site where her parents died in Litzmannstadt. The Morelli sisters never returned to Italy to visit their relatives. Lessa and Sofia didn't really like the hamantashen – it wasn't sweet enough – but they loved the fact that somebody baked for them. Somehow their friendship with Sora Banka made them feel special, maybe because she was from the other side of town or because when she came to visit she wore nice dresses and brought baked goods. Or maybe because Sora Banka never asked them for anything; she came bearing gifts and left empty-handed. Lessa always offered to pack her up some meatballs or manicotti or chicken soup – "for your family" – but Sora graciously declined. The Holocaust was only a few decades past at the time, and yet the only thing Lessa and Sofia knew about Sora Banka was that she was married to a doctor, made oddly shaped pastry, and was a Jew, which in some way made her special. Whenever Lessa introduced her friend to one of the grandchildren she would say: "This is Sora Banka. She's Jewish."

If the occupants of 59 Lehigh Lane understood little about religion and non-secular sweet goods, they grasped even less about politics and policymaking. Everybody knew the name of the sitting President of the United States and the first name of the current Geneva Mayor, and that was about it. Mayor Louis Erman was a regular at the Morelli's bar every Friday night for all eight of his years in office. He sat on the last stool closest to the dining room and flirted with all the waitresses and greeted the dinner guests as they passed through the bar on the way to their tables. Behind his back his constituents called him "Electric Arm," because his right arm would automatically extend every time someone's hand came close enough for him to shake. After his third or fourth highball he would stagger into the kitchen and ask, "What's good tonight?" That was Lessa's prompt to pack up a giant portion of spaghetti or ravioli or lasagna with a couple of meatballs or sausages, which His Honor paid for with a sloppy kiss on the cheek. Most likely over the years the family got its money's worth in political subtleties that came with certain benefits. Like the time Gus wanted to expand the main parking lot on the north side of the restaurant but was rebuffed because of an abutment restriction.

"Abutment my ass," Gus screamed at no one in particular. "Call the goddamn judge." He always referred to Mayor Erman as the "goddamn judge," although he was not a judge and never even studied law.

Another time might have been when Nick was briefly incarcerated as a teenager for disorderly conduct in the parking lot by the lake. Although he was released within an hour to his grandmother's custody, it was nevertheless an official arrest, and Sergeant Mickey, at the time, told them his name would have to appear in the next Police Blotter, which was published weekly in the local newspaper. "We'll see about that," Lessa snorted under her breath as they left the station that night. Sure enough, Nick's name never appeared in print with the other delinquents, degenerates, and drunks. It was a busy week for petty crimes in Geneva and the alphabetic list of perps was long. Nick's name should have been posted between Jeffrey Polito and Stephen Porter. The sequence should have been "Jeffrey Polito, Nicholas Poole, Stephen Porter." But there was no "Nicholas Poole." Not in the newspaper. Not that day. The editor of the newspaper was a regular at Morelli's.

CHAPTER THIRTEEN
Camelot Falls

Rarely a consensus on any topic of discussion could be reached in the back room at Morelli's. The people there argued about everything from religion to food to people, places, and things. They argued about politics and politicians although they knew very little about those subjects. Their political agenda was based on the day's headlines in the local newspaper or The Racing Form, whether it was a downtown zoning issue or a bill before the United States Senate or the horses running in the seventh at Aqueduct Racetrack in Queens, New York. All they needed to start an argument was for someone to read a headline aloud. Then everybody had an opinion.

There was a single exception to the incessant bickering. When it came to John Fitzgerald Kennedy, the thirty-fifth President of the United States, the entire Morelli's contingent was staunchly of one mind: the man was a saint. He was young, handsome, and charismatic. He had a glamorous and charming wife. JFK was Irish, and that made him more respectable than politicians of other descents, even Italians. He was Catholic, so he got the whole God thing right. He was the leader of the free world and on his watch, people felt safe and sound. He wasn't a Democrat or a Republican. He was JFK.

Friday, November 22, 1963 was an unseasonably warm fall day in upstate New York. The grammar school – Saint Thomas Aquinas – was dismissed just after lunchtime when the principal, Sister Regina, made an announcement over the PA system; her voice was uncharacteristically slow and sad. Her normal daily broadcasts were fast and booming. Someone had been shot, is what Dennis made of the message, and it must have been someone important for the sister to suddenly cancel school. As soon as Dennis got outside he felt the warm air on his face, so he took off his jacket. There were buses and cars in the parking lot waiting to take students home. Parents had been alerted of the early dismissal. Dennis and Nick lived close enough to the school to walk, but on this day they weren't going home. They were headed to 59 Lehigh Lane to stay with their grandmother until their mother finished work at LoMoro's. By the time they got to Morelli's Dennis had lost his jacket and knew for sure he would be sent back to find it. "I'm not going back with you, you shithead," Nick scolded. "Better find it or Ma's gonna kick your ass."

At around 12:30PM that day, President Kennedy was struck by one bullet in the neck and another in the head as his motorcade drove through downtown Dallas, Texas. He was pronounced dead shortly after arriving at a nearby hospital.

Nick, a third grader at the time, knew as soon as he entered through the back door – the family's door – at 59 Lehigh Lane that something was different; different in a bad way. There was no one in the kitchen cooking for the hungry customers who would be showing up in a couple of hours. The stoves were cold, and the room was dark. Usually at this time of day the kitchen was hectic, loud, and bright, like the inside of a train station at rush hour. There were a few people sitting around the table in the back room, but the usual cacophony was replaced with an eerie calm. There was no talking. One woman was crying. Everyone was somber. Lessa was not there to greet the boys like always. Someone said she was upstairs resting, in her bedroom. Lessa Donato never took naps during the middle of the day. This had something to do with Sister Regina's announcement on the PA system back in school. Nick wished he had paid closer attention.

Nick walked into the parlor to find several older ladies with teary eyes watching Walter Cronkite on the grainy black & white 21-inch RCA TV. He was reporting on what was officially now the JFK assassination. There was Giulia Harraka, Joan DeMattis, Lucy Ritaneo, Cloris Morris, Amalia Penbad, Mary Felice, and Margie Testa. Some kept house, some rolled meatballs, some washed dishes. In a pinch they could work the salad station or plate desserts. They were always around and willing to do whatever was asked of them. They were unheralded but not unappreciated. And they never asked for anything beyond their regular wages, which were paid from the cash that Lessa and Sofia kept stuffed in pockets in their cooking smocks. These women were not particularly close. They considered themselves co-workers or acquaintances more than friends. They did not congregate outside of Morelli's. But on that day, they mourned together like they all lost the same father.

Giulia Harraka, the wrinkly old Romanian woman who washed the restaurant dishes every night and carried out the garbage in a big tin bucket every half-hour, was sitting closest to the TV and sobbing the most visibly. It looked like she was hanging onto every word that came from Cronkite's mouth, even though she could not understand a word of English, from what anyone knew. Nick was only eight years old but just then he began to realize the profound influence that JFK had on the people of the nation, regardless of their native language.

In the days and weeks that followed there would be stories about how people reacted to the death of President Kennedy. Teachers falling to their knees in the middle of class, factory workers walking off their shifts like zombies, a traffic cop who heard the news from a driver and halted traffic for his own personal moment of silence. Mothers hugging confused children, grown men crying openly in their offices, in restaurants, on golf courses. But there could not have been a sincerer outpouring of emotion than what transpired in the Morelli's parlor that day by a group of people who more than likely did not even vote in the general election, and who probably knew even less about Kennedy's Camelot than they did about Homer's Ancient Greece. Not a person in Morelli's on that dismal day in November 1963, nor on the days immediately after, spoke a single word of anger or vengeance toward the assassin Lee Harvey Oswald, nor of his own assassination at the hands of Jack Ruby. They showed only great sadness and remorse over the loss of their beloved President. They were inconsolable.

On so many fronts the 1960s were a complex span of years. They have been described as the best of times and the worst of times. The sixties were known as a watershed decade. Groundbreaking. America experienced a surge in nuclear power, the blossoming of flower power, and the influence of Black Power, all representative of a tumultuous zeitgeist. There was a race to space and riots over race. Americans were blessed with great leaders like John and Robert Kennedy and Martin Luther King, who all possessed splendid vision and noble intentions that never fully came to fruition during their earthly time.

In 1961 the Germans built a wall to physically and politically separate East and West Berliners. The Berlin Wall came down in 1989 and its remnants now serve as souvenirs around the world. In 1964 Americans constructed the world's first roofed sports stadium in Houston, Texas. After a prosperous forty-year run the Astrodome sits vacant. People must have figured baseball was best played under a summer sky.

In 1965 the first American combat troops landed in Vietnam to fight a war that would last ten years, and that many people would never come to understand. Four years later three men landed on the moon and took one giant leap. The entire trip from launch to splash down lasted about eight days. It would be called "humanity's greatest achievement in space." To many, it was never clear what purpose it served other than to meet JFK's 1961 quest to beat the Soviets to the moon, and maybe pave the way for satellite TV and GPS navigation.

In 1968 The Beatles released "The White Album," a double set of vinyl records in a plain white sleeve with no graphics or text other than the band's name embossed across the front cover. The songs were said to reflect the conflicting political and social emotions of the sixties. Some critics called it the greatest album of all time, and it was believed that the making of this album was so stressful and important that it led to the breakup of the greatest band of all time. This was profound stuff. Be that as it may, someone told Dennis that underneath the white paper layer on the jacket was a photograph of a naked girl, so he busted open his ceramic bank, pinched a few more bucks from his mother's purse and paid a whopping $10.94 for the album at the record store on Keuka Street. He did a fucking Helter-Skelter on that album jacket and did not see even a single pink nipple.

A lot of important events took place in the 1960s that seemed paradoxical at the time. A tenet of the decade was that people were separate but equal. What did that mean? It was a decade of social and cultural liberation. What about the families of the three civil rights workers murdered in Mississippi in 1964? How equal did they feel? How liberated did the patrons of the Stonewall Inn, a predominantly gay night club in New York City's Greenwich Village, feel when cops raided the place in the early hours of June 28, 1969? That same year Woodstock, the music festival that defined an entire generation, was taking place about three hours from where Morelli's served dinner every night, yet the people in the back room didn't know Joan Baez from Joan of Arc.

Amazingly, the New York Mets won the World Series in 1969 by defeating the Baltimore Orioles in five games. New York City, which two months earlier held a ticker-tape parade to honor the Apollo 11 astronauts who walked on the moon, similarly celebrated the baseball feat of its team from Flushing, Queens. If you were a Yankees fan you didn't care anything about the New York Mets. Or ticker-tape parades.

The most vivid and lasting memories of that decade were the ones that Walter Cronkite presided over on his nightly TV broadcast. He was always so calm and steady even when the people watching him were sad or happy or angry. While people were confused, he was sure and decisive. He was reassuring. Somewhere between John Kennedy's assassination and Neil Armstrong's lunar stroll, probably half the male baby boomers at the time made up their minds to become television reporters. By the time Watergate rolled around, the Cronkite wannabes were taking journalism classes as college freshmen.

Nicky Poole wandered into the sixties as a guileless five-year-old missing one front tooth, and by the time the decade came to its end, the deep and historical events that took place over those ten years barely altered his innocent indifference. He watched Cronkite report on Vietnam but didn't know anyone who left home to fight in a war, nor anyone who returned home after serving in one. The evening news was filled with film of race riots, but some of Nick's best friends were African Americans, and they had cute sisters. Cronkite showed pictures from around the country of people breaking store windows and setting fires. Edie took Dennis and Nick for dungarees and underwear at a department store in a shopping center on the other side of town, and its windows were always clean and filled with smartly dressed mannequins. There were no fires.

CHAPTER FOURTEEN

Mary Lou the Magnificent

That's not to say the 1960s were totally wasted on young boys of the time. There was another revolution taking place. Not in the fields of Southeast Asia or on the streets of Newark, New Jersey, or Detroit or in the Watts neighborhood of Los Angeles. It wasn't the British music invasion. This revolution took place inside the souls of men and women throughout the western world. It was a revolution that challenged traditional sexual protocols and interpersonal relationships. Couples were swinging and swapping. Sex was premarital. We had "The Pill." Hippies. Miniskirts. Free love and love-ins, and a Broadway play called "Hair" which, as Dennis explained to his younger brother, was all about removing your clothes in public. The 1960s introduced a counterculture of ideals and ethics. The sexual liberation included homosexuality. The Poole boys? They liked girls. Especially beautiful girls on posters wearing almost nothing.

One of their fondest memories of the sixties was the proliferation of pornography in the movies. Back then it was easy to sneak into The Stars Theater on Keuka Street to watch adult-rated films. The theater had a side door in an alley that adults rarely walked through because it was dark, littered with broken glass and smelled like urine. The door was always left open a crack to let the air in since the theater had no air conditioning in the hot summer months, and in the winter the heat ran full blast, which made it uncomfortably clammy. Dennis, Nick and their pals would peek through the crack, and as soon as the usher walked by while making his rounds, they'd slip into the nearest empty seats.

Nick was twelve when he saw The Graduate and his very first set of tits. They belonged to Anne Bancroft, who played Mrs. Robinson, or so Nick thought. Later in life he would read that they used stand-ins for all the nude scenes in the movie. It didn't make any difference to him. They would always be Mrs. Robinson's tits. The tits appeared on screen only briefly, maybe for a second, in the scene where Mrs. Robinson was seducing a young and timid Ben Braddock, played by Dustin Hoffman, in her bedroom. Nevertheless, they are the tits Nick remembered second most vividly from his youth.

The breasts most indelibly etched on his brain were the property of Mary Lou Malloy. She was named after her maternal grandmother, Mary, and paternal grandfather, Louis. Nobody called her just "Mary" or just "Lou." She was "Mary Lou." It was the summer of 1967, which history would remember as "The Summer of Love" in reference to the social spectacle that put San Francisco's Haight-Ashbury neighborhood on the map when one hundred thousand hippies gathered there to make love, not war. Nick didn't know anything about Haight-Ashbury back then, and if the people in the back room at Morelli's were correct, a "goddamned hippie" was anyone a day late for a haircut. But he was learning about sex and he had Mrs. Robinson and Mary Lou Malloy to thank for that. Mary Lou was only thirteen, a year older than Nick, yet her sinuous figure contradicted her young age. Her face was white and smooth with tiny pinkish freckles that harmonized perfectly with the strawberry blonde hair on her head, and in other places that would eventually be made known to Nick. She had pleasantly zaftig hips that transitioned impeccably into her long, slender legs – also milky white and smooth. There was nothing subliminal about his attraction; it was true love. Mary Lou Malloy was Nick's pin-up girl, and the reason for much of his adolescent angst.

Mary Lou was not only biologically superior to the other girls in the neighborhood, she was also savvy in the ways of the world. She had gravitas. And cleavage. She painted her toenails. Her ambition was to become a nurse. She worked as a Candy Striper at the hospital in Geneva, and while she genuinely liked serving the greater good, she also liked the status of having a job, even if it did not pay a wage. It was fitting that she was the only one of her peers to have a job. Then again, Mary Lou had no peers.

On Monday, Wednesday and Friday mornings during the summer of sixty-seven, Nick would sit on his front porch and wait for her to walk by on her way to work wearing what he imagined to be nothing at all beneath her red-and-white striped pinafore. He made flirtatious remarks like "nice apron," and she would respond with a smile or a wave. One day, it was a Friday, he came up with a new, totally spontaneous line as she walked past. "Wanna play doctor?" The question just spilled from his mouth with no forethought or calculation. It was completely out of character for him. But as surprised as he was by his own query, Mary Lou's comeback knocked him for a loop. Without hesitation, in mid stride, she gave Nick a wink and said, "I'm ready if you are."

He nearly pissed in his pants just thinking about it. She wore a uniform and worked in a hospital. She was halfway to becoming a real nurse. For all Nick knew she was already having sex with doctors. By comparison, Nick still crawled under the bed when he heard thunder.

Nick had no idea whether the notion of playing doctor with Mary Lou that day or any other day would come to fulfilment, but if it were to happen, he damn sure wanted some experience before he stripped down to his skivvies in front of a girl. Nick always giggled when Dr. Dooley squeezed his privates during his annual physicals. He did not want to giggle should Mary Lou Malloy exercise the traditional cup-and-cough procedure.

Nick thought about asking Dennis for some advice since he at least had a little experience playing doctor with a few of the other kids in the neighborhood, but on second thought he recalled that the incident did not end well for his older brother. The "medical staff," which included friends Harold Durso, Carol Petter, Fat Freddy Kaminsky, Stephanie Coons, Artie Pierce, Bobby Corcoran and, of course, Leo Lusco – a quirky kid who was game for anything, anytime, anywhere with no questions asked and no fear of reprisal – used Vicks VapoRub to lubricate the thermometer before they inserted it into Dennis's rectum. As a lube it worked fine, but unfortunately it stung like a thousand pin pricks and caused Dennis to jump so violently that the thermometer completely disappeared up his asshole. He hopped around in gyrations, fanning his fiery backside with both hands, desperately seeking relief. "It burns! It burns! It burns! It burns!" he whined on. "Oh my god it burns it burns it burns it burns! Somebody do something! It burns! It burns! It burns!"

Most of the kids scattered in disgust. Not Leo. Leo never ran from trouble, not even a blazing butthole. "Try shitting it out!" he yelled as he followed Dennis around in circles. "Try shitting it out!" Leo was always thinking outside the box. At one of the seances the neighborhood kids held on random summer nights when they couldn't think of anything better to do, it was Leo who suggested to raise Marilyn Monroe so he could see her boobies. As dumb as it sounded, no one argued.

Dennis ran into the house where Nick was sitting in front of the TV watching an episode of The Little Rascals and eating a bowl of cereal. He turned his back to Nick, pulled his pants back down, bent over and shoved his ass in his brother's face. Nick was stunned, speechless. He had no idea what any of this meant, though he did know enough to immediately move his face and his breakfast away from the inflamed sphincter.

Leo followed Dennis into the house in very short order and explained the situation.

"It went all the way up there?" Nick asked in astonishment.

"Yep. The whole thing. Went right up his ass. You can barely see the end of it. I told him to shit it out."

Dennis still had his ass pointed at his brother's face, and Nick was concerned that a fart could easily send the pointy projectile hurling directly through his eyeball.

"Shit it out? That's a stupid idea," Nick said, quickly moving out of the line of fire.

"Then what should he do?" Leo asked.

By now Dennis was dragging his ass across the kitchen floor trying to cool it down on the linoleum, unaware that he was only pushing the foreign object further into his asshole. "Quick Nicky, pull it out with your fingers," he pleaded.

"No fucking way," Nick screeched.

"What am I going to do?" Dennis whined.

"Shit it out! Shit it out!" Leo yelled again. "Maybe eat some prunes. My mother eats prunes when she wants to shit."

"I'm gonna get Mom," Nick volunteered. He knew Dennis would likely be punished for his exploits and be interminably embarrassed when their mother confronted the other parents, and Nick was elated to take that risk. Besides, their mother, who had been sleeping when all this began same as most mornings following a long night behind the stove at Morelli's, was getting up and about amid all the commotion. She yelled from her bedroom, "What the Christ is going on down there?"

"Dennis was playing doctor with his friends and got a thermometer stuck up his ass," Nick responded without punctuation.

There was a second of silence that felt more like a minute, and then came their mother's reply: "Did he try shitting it out?"

They all ended up in Dr. Dooley's office that morning. Dennis could no longer sit so he had to lay ass up in the back seat while Nick and Leo sat up front with Edie.

"Leo, you don't have to come to the doctor with us," Edie said. She was quite fond of Leo, but it was no secret to anybody that he annoyed her to no end. "Your mother might be wondering where you are."

"Oh no, Mrs. Poole. I should go with you, so I'll know what to do the next time this happens, and we won't have to bother you," Leo replied, most sincerely.

Nick and Leo never got to see the actual extraction; they stayed in the waiting room while Edie and Dennis went in to see Dr. Dooley. When they came out, Dr. Dooley held up a plastic bag containing the tainted thermometer, glared at Nick and Leo, and said, curtly, "Next time you nitwits can pull this out yourselves. Use your teeth for all I care. I have sick people to take care of."

"What would you have done if I was still working in the butcher shop, and wasn't here when this happened?" Edie asked the boys on the ride home. A moment of thoughtful silence, and then, "Wouldn't he have to shit it out sooner or later?" Leo replied. "Can I have it back? The thermometer? I have to put it back in my mother's medicine cabinet."

As it turned out, Nick never did meet up with Mary Lou after her shift at the hospital that Friday in the summer of 1967. He made himself scarce when all he could think of was losing a thermometer up her ass, or worse, up his own ass. But he would get another chance before the end of the decade.

Besides a real job, a figure, and boobs, Mary Lou had something else the other girls in the neighborhood did not have: a steady boyfriend. It was 1968 and Nick was thirteen. Mary Lou was fourteen, same age as her boyfriend, Gordy Vogel. Even though he was a year older than Nick, Gordy was in the same grade at school and probably should have been even further back. He was borderline illiterate, socially impaired and had no business with a girl like Mary Lou, but he did have the suggestion of a mustache and a few long, wiry hairs on each side of his face that could have been mistaken for sideburns. He also had a job helping his father build sheds, porches, closets and other small structures as well as doing general handy work and household repairs, so, unlike the other boys, he could afford to take a girl on a date. Maybe Mary Lou figured he was more biologically advanced then the rest of the boys around her. Maybe Gordy was the only boy around her with the man-balls to make a move. The best Nick could do was to throw down a cheesy line and then hide under his bed.

But all that changed on July 4, 1968. Gordy was on a camping trip with the other Vogel inbreeds. A group of the boys were playing Acey-Deucy on the wooden picnic table at Soldier's Playground on North Walnut Street. Two cards are dealt face-up to one player, who then bets from zero up to the total amount of money that is in the pot at the time whether the third card will numerically fall in between the first two. If the third card fell in between the two up cards, the punter would take the amount he bet out of the pot; if the third card fell outside of the two up cards, he would "burn" and have to add what he bet to the pot. An ace and a deuce, of course, gave the player the best odds of winning, but not guaranteed since another ace or deuce could come up. Ties lost. The players anteed fifty cents each to start the game, and after a dozen or so hands the pot was up to $48 because there were several burns in a row. Nick drew a king and a two on his turn, the second-best odds to win after an ace and a deuce, and he would have bet the total amount in the pot but had only $8 to his name. He tried to borrow $40 to match the pot in return for a cut of the winnings, a common practice in the game, but got no takers. All the boys had already contributed to the pot and no one wanted to see Nick walk away with everything. They were greedy that way. Just when Nick was about to make his

$8 bet, Mary Lou, who never took part in the game herself, came up behind him. "I'll back Nicky for the pot," she announced.

"Yeah? Show us the money," Johnny DiPadova protested. A few hands earlier he was burned on a queen - three and was the most heavily vested in the pot. Challenging a backer, or anyone betting a pot as large as $48, became protocol after the time Marty Scher went for it all on a $35 pot and did not have the cash to fork over when he got burned on an ace - deuce. Mary Lou slid her hand into the back pocket of her incredibly short cut-off jeans and withdrew four neatly creased $10 bills.

"How's this?" she asked. Before Nick could even accept her offer – he was a little stunned that she showed up out of nowhere, that she had $40 cash on hand, and that he could see the side of her ass cheek when she lifted the bills out of her back pocket – the dealer turned over a six of spades and slapped it down between the king and the two. There were a lot of grunts and groans, but the only sound Nick heard was Mary Lou whispering in his ear, "Take our money and let's get out of here." The game was going to break up anyway since he was the only one with enough money left to bet, so he collected the $48 from the center of the picnic table and walked away with the dismantling group, including Mary Lou. They all separated exiting the playground, walking generally toward their respective homes. At some point it was just Mary Lou and Nick, walking side by side.

"What's my share?" she asked, more playful than business-like.

"How much you want?"

"I don't know. Let's go to my house and get something to drink. We can figure it out there."

"Where'd you get $40?"

"My father. I'm supposed to get groceries today," Mary Lou said.

"What if we lost?"

"You and me would have to run away together," she answered with a wink, the same wink Nick remembered from a year ago when he asked her to play doctor. Mary Lou had a cocksure answer for everything. She never dithered. Never hemmed or hawed.

It was oppressively hot and humid that day. Mary Lou pulled a couple of tall glasses from the top shelf in the kitchen cupboard and filled them with ice cubes. Again, Nick got a good look at her ass cheeks when she reached for the glasses. She took one of the cubes and wiped it across her forehead, then plunked it back into her glass. She poured cherry Kool-Aid into each of the glasses until they flowed over. Mary Lou sipped from her glass and the sweet red nectar dripped easily down her chin, onto her freckled chest and between her rounded breasts. It stained her shirt. Nick was close enough to smell her cherry-flavored sweat.

"Wait here," she said. "I have to change my shirt."

Nick was completely engulfed in the eroticism of the moment. Pulsating, feverish. He considered his next move. A girl like Mary Lou, he figured, would want a man that took charge, not a boy that drank Kool-Aid from a straw. He quickly threw his straw into the trash. The next move would have to be his, and he would have to take his game up a few ticks.

But what happened next exceeded his wildest masturbatory fantasies. It was way too late for him to do anything with his own game. Mary Lou had elevated things to a sexually ethereal plateau. She walked back into the kitchen wearing only a white terrycloth bathrobe that was untied around the waist, and a New York Yankee baseball cap that inexplicably made her ten times sexier than if she weren't wearing it. Under the robe she was completely naked. The first thing Nick noticed after the baseball cap were her boobs. He was no expert, but these boobs must have won awards. They were perfectly symmetrical. Round yet firm. Firm yet supple. If they were people, they would have been identical twins. His eyes drifted slowly down her body until he fixed his gaze on the money shot: a triangular patch of silky, reddish pubic hair. Mary Lou was finely crafted from top to bottom. Her toenails were painted the same color as her fingernails.

Nick thought things were going smashingly, this being his maiden encounter with a naked girl. All he had to do was stand there with his mouth closed and try not to look like this was, in fact, his maiden encounter with a naked girl. Then Mary Lou spoke just six words that took him from a totally euphoric state to such tremendous anxiety he felt a sharp pain in the pit of his stomach.

"Let's go up to my room," she said.

Nick gave her a confused look but knew exactly what she meant. She had a body like one of the pin-up girls in Vinny's bedroom, and he had a body like Alfalfa, one of the Little Rascals he watched on TV on Saturday mornings. It never occurred to him that he would have to take his clothes off to have sex with a girl. In his fantasies only the girl was naked. As he instantly recalled every R-rated movie he watched at The Stars Theater – starting with The Graduate – he could not remember seeing even one nude man. He was sure only the women were naked in all the sex scenes. He was not prepared for this. More than likely he wasn't even wearing clean underwear. Despite all his mother's warnings, he never thought he'd be hit by a car while crossing the street.

"Right now? Lemme finish my Kool-Aid," Nick said, stalling. "Hey, I didn't know you were a Yankee fan. Who's your favorite player? Gotta be the Mick, right? I think this is his last year though. Can hardly run anymore. Probably move Pepitone to first. He's ok. But ain't no Mick."

Ignoring his trepidation, or maybe amused by it, or possibly even bored by it, Mary Lou led Nick up the stairs to her bedroom. "What if someone comes home?" he asked. "Shouldn't we go somewhere more private?" He was thinking somewhere with less light. Like a cave. Or the trunk of a car. If he were to take off his clothes, he did not want it to be in the full light of day. Not so that Mary Lou could examine his body like he examined hers. She was ripe and lush. He was gaunt and pale.

Mary Lou left her robe on, but untethered. She sensed things were moving a little fast for Nick. She was experienced that way. He wondered what she saw in someone like him in the first place. He didn't have the swagger – or the facial hair – that Gordy Vogel had. Nick figured he was more athletic than Gordy, but Mary Lou was not interested in sports. He was an Honor Roll student, and was already learning Spanish, but Mary Lou, though street smart, was not the intellectual type either. They did have proximity going for them. They lived on the same block; virtually grew up together, playing in their backyards, in sand boxes, on swing sets. They saw each other almost every day as far back as either could remember, until she left their Catholic elementary school after sixth grade to attend a public middle school. She was the only child of a single father – she never talked about her mother. Nick and Mary Lou, for most of their young lives together, were like a brother and sister until puberty screwed everything up. But even now there was a certain comfort between them. Maybe that was the attraction. Nick was familiar. He was safe. He was unknowing but teachable.

The next hour or so did not go anything like Nick imagined it would. Mary Lou was not the sex-seeking seductress with a rapacious sexual appetite that had him quaking in his black Converse hi-tops when she walked into the kitchen wearing only her robe and a baseball cap. To the contrary, she was charming and thoughtful. As they were sitting on her bed, just talking, he reminded himself that this girl had known him all his life. She saw him coming and going on most days. She knew his schedule; she knew his friends and most likely knew he had never been alone with a girl before. Not like this. For the first time he could see that Mary Lou was deep. He could see she had real feelings for him. And he could see her right nipple poking out of the opening in her robe. Which brought him back to the matter at hand.

They talked about sex for a while. Mary Lou did most of the talking. She told Nick what girls liked and did not like. He was way off on both counts. She gave him some hands-on training. He paid very close attention to everything she did and said. At some point he was wearing only his underwear. Fortunately, they turned out to be reasonably clean. She let him feel her breasts as she explained the difference between fiddling and fondling, nuances that to Nick were not immediately distinct. They practiced French kissing; his only previous experience was when he played spin the bottle at an eighth-grade graduation party a few weeks earlier and Carol Mitchell slipped him her tongue. Mary Lou said he was a pretty good kisser. The lesson ended abruptly two seconds after Mary Lou placed her hand over the bulge on the front of Nick's white BVDs. At first, he was embarrassed, but Mary Lou, like she had done for the entire time they were together that afternoon, was comforting, in a very natural kind of way. She displayed incredible seriousness for a girl of fourteen. They talked for several more minutes, about nothing important, before getting dressed. "Snap my bra," she said unemotionally. Another first for Nick.

"I'm hungry," she said. "How 'bout you buy us a pizza with that money you won today?"

They didn't see much of each other for the rest of that summer. Gordy came back from camping and picked up again with Mary Lou. She quit her job at the hospital and started working in a laundromat downtown, folding clothes for an actual paycheck. On the couple of occasions she and Nick crossed paths there was no tension whatsoever. They made mostly playful chatter, but he knew they were thinking the same thought. For him it was a very pleasant thought. He liked to think it was for her as well. Either way, there was chemistry.

Nick entered high school that fall with a sense of confidence that was lacking before. He was a tougher athlete. He raised his hand more in class. He paid attention to where his hair was parted and how his clothes fit. When he talked to a girl he kept his head up, not down to his shoes. There may have been a swagger in his step. It was like he walked through the front doors of the high school with a purpose, instead of being unaware. Nick was sure that the time he spent with Mary Lou in her bedroom that summer day had something to do with his newfound hubris.

By the next summer, Mary Lou had moved to Florida to live with her grandmother. It was sudden; Nick never said goodbye. Soon after she left there was talk around the neighborhood that she went away to have a baby. It was even a hot topic in the back room at Morelli's. Her father, from time to time, did odd jobs for the restaurant, so there was a connection, and a pregnant teenager was textbook fodder for the rumor mill. Nick didn't believe it. Mary Lou was too sex-savvy to let that happen to her, at least accidentally. And he knew she had much bigger plans for herself than to become a teenage mother. On top of that, if she were pregnant, the baby would have likely been the spawn of Gordy Vogel. At the very least she should have been knocked up by a male nurse, if not a doctor or surgeon.

Years later Nick ran into a mutual friend from their Soldier's Playground days in an airport. It was a stormy night and they had time to catch up over a few drinks while their flights were delayed. The friend had heard, but could not confirm, that Mary Lou was still living in Florida and was married. He did not know whether she had any children. Or whether she had married a doctor.

CHAPTER FIFTEEN

Double Shifts and Daily Doubles

The late 1960s and early 1970s ushered in a time of great growth and opportunity for Morelli's. The restaurant was packed on Friday and Saturday nights. People who came in for dinner without a reservation waited at the bar for an hour, so the bar business was also brisk. The old ice-making machine in the basement beneath the bar really had to chug to keep up with the highball and rocks orders on weekends. Dennis was carrying the ice up from the basement on weekends now to earn a few bucks, and he suggested that it might be time to buy a new machine. Gus, who ran the bar, shot back with his usual vitriol, "Ice machine my ass. Just keep filling them goddamn buckets."

There were three bartenders working weekend nights, even though there was barely room for two of them to maneuver productively behind the bar. The dining room was also crowded with waitresses to keep up with the steady stream of customers, but unlike the lumbering bartenders, these ladies glided between and betwixt the maze of square tables like a professional dance troupe. The prima donna was a two-hundred-thirty-pound waitress named Olivia Lombardi, who was as wide as she was tall. Despite her tremendous girth and clunky looking orthopedic shoes, Olivia earned the nickname "Twinkle Toes" for the way she sashayed from table to table, balancing trays stacked with countless plates of food on one hand and a shoulder. All the Morelli's waitresses were on their feet from six to 10PM on weekend nights. Every night as her shift was winding down, Olivia, no matter how exhausted, would belt out her trademark tune – "Mambo Italiano" – for the dwindling crowd. Everyone still in the bar would join those in the dining room to sing the most memorable lines:

"And hey Mambo! Don't want to tarantella,
Hey Mambo! No more-a moozzarella.
Hey Mambo! Hey Mambo Italiano.
Try an enchilada with a fish-a-barcalada ..."

The restaurant became so popular that the owners decided to open at noon for lunch on Sundays. Lunch at Morelli's was served family style – large plates of food holding multiple portions to be shared around the entire table. It quickly became the "in thing" to do on Sunday afternoons throughout the Finger Lakes. The bartenders, waitresses, cooks, and dishwashers showed up for work at eleven in the morning and left at about four in the afternoon, which made it an even longer shift than the regular dinner service. The restaurant closed from four to five to set up for dinner. Some of the waitresses stayed for a double shift.

The dinner crowds on Monday through Thursday were not as heavy as the weekends, but business was still steady. Dennis made less ice runs from the basement to the bar on these nights, but the machine still had to run full throttle to keep up. One of the bartenders had the idea to keep all the bottled booze in the coolers with the beer so that they could use less ice in the cocktails. It seemed to work.

Everyone was paid well when they worked, and they were always working. Suppliers who came in to sell their products usually left smiling. This presented another opportunity for Dennis and Nick to earn a few bucks, and probably get their asses kicked once again for screwing something up. There were always crates of produce and boxes of meats stacked on the kitchen floor that needed to be hauled into the crowded walk-in cooler. Fifty-six-ounce No. 5 cans of whole and crushed tomatoes, six to a case, had to be carried down a steep, creaky set of wooden steps to the small basement below the kitchen. Each case weighed twenty-one pounds. Five-gallon rounds of ice cream and Spumoni had to be lifted into the well freezer in the back room. Smaller desserts, like cannoli and tortoni cups, were stored in the stand-up freezer, also in the back room. Sometimes the stand-up freezer was so crammed with frost and food that the door would only close by the force of a full body slam, causing a few of the desserts to crack or crush. It was no use asking to have the freezer defrosted. "Defrost my ass," Gus would say. "Just get that shit in there before it melts."

By the end of 1974 Morelli's Restaurant was being run by the two widowed sisters – Lessa Donato and Sofia Riotto. Lessa's husband, Salvatore, died a few years earlier after a long illness. At the time, his service was believed to be the most attended in the history of Luhmann's Funeral Home on Pultney Street, although many of the mourners were not from the Geneva area but rather from the five boroughs of New York City. He was fifty-six. When Sal died,

Lessa, Sofia and Gus decided to close the small grocery store on Castle Street that he co-owned with a friend – it served mostly as a gambling parlor – to concentrate on the restaurant.

Gus Morelli died one day before Thanksgiving in 1974. He suffered a massive coronary at the Mare-Do-Well Racetrack. He went to the track every day and didn't start his day in the restaurant until the bar opened at 4PM. He thought of the track as his day job. In fact, every morning when he left for the track he would announce, "I'm going to work." He took it seriously.

Gus usually drove to the track alone, but on this day Lessa went with him even though the day before Thanksgiving was one of the busiest days of the year at the restaurant. The night before, Tuesday, several of her late husband's New York City cronies came into the restaurant for dinner. They had just purchased two thoroughbreds; one was scheduled to run in the first race at Mare-Do-Well on Wednesday, the other in the second race. Before leaving the restaurant, one of the men, Whammy LaDuca, handed Lessa a piece of paper with the writing: 4 fst 7 snd. "Tomorrow," he whispered in her ear. Lessa understood that she should bet the number four horse in the first race and the number seven horse in the second race at Mare-Do-Well the next day. If they both finished first in their respective races it would be a Daily Double, which would pay exponentially higher than any single race winner. She knew LaDuca well enough to know she should take heed. He had given her husband tips in the past and while she never knew the outcome of the bets, she remembered how Sal would rush to the track every time he heard from or met with LaDuca. His rap sheet included a number of attempts to influence the outcome of horse races from Florida up to Massachusetts, for each of which he did little or no time other than probation. His expertise in such areas is probably what kept him in the good graces of the group from New York City, since he did not appear to have much else to offer.

On the morning of the races Lessa grabbed The Racing Form from under Gus's gander and perused Mare-Do-Well's first two races of the day, which would account for the Daily Double. She fancied herself a capable thoroughbred handicapper, even though her career winnings would not bear that out. She saw that the two horses LaDuca picked were longshots – "dogs," she muttered to herself as she slapped The Racing Form back down in front of Gus, barely missing his morning plate of two eggs sunny side up, four strips of crispy bacon and a couple pieces of burnt toast dripping with salty butter.

"What the Christ are you bitching about?" Gus sneered, barely looking up from the paper. "Can't you see I'm trying to work here?" He also thought himself to be a skillful handicapper, but his winning percentage proposed otherwise.

LaDuca's picks were not the horses owned by the men at the restaurant the night before. The horses they owned, in fact, were the favorites in each of the first two races, according to The Racing Form. That confused Lessa, but also convinced her to bet the Daily Double that was scribbled on the slip of paper. Something was so obviously strange with LaDuca's picks that Lessa was compelled to bet them as he instructed. She couldn't ask Gus to run the bet to the track for her because he had a rule not to place bets for anyone but himself. He was a very superstitious gambler and believed that any horse he bet on that he did not pick on his own would jinx his horse. Her only other option was to send the bet with Angelo, the cigarette salesman, but she figured he would share the tip with all his connections and possibly make the betting line suspicious.

Angelo was not a very good salesman; he carried the most popular cigarette and cigar brands that bars had to stock as a matter of course so, really, he just took orders and loaded the two machines, one in the restaurant near the hostess stand and the other in the bar. He stacked a few packs of each brand behind the bar in case the machines went down, or the cash register was low on change. He made his money taking bets and he always took a cut of the winnings, the amount he surreptitiously determined on his own, generally the bigger the win the bigger the slice. No one complained because when he cashed winning tickets that paid enough to require a Social Security number for tax purposes, Angelo did not deduct for taxes. There was speculation that he had someone on the other side of the cashier's window who took a few bucks to pay the winning tickets off the books. Or perhaps the ne'er-do-well just didn't pay taxes at all.

On top of all that, Lessa simply did not want this man to prosper in any way from her tip. When Angelo saw Lessa leaving for the track with Gus on a day when she usually would not have left the restaurant, he figured she had something up her sleeve.

LaDuca's scam came off perfectly. It was never established exactly how he did it. Maybe he bribed a few greedy jockeys to allow the longshots to beat the field. Maybe the horses were tampered with or drugged or switched altogether. In the 1970s New York racetracks routinely flouted handicapping rationale. Jockeys figured out that they could make more money betting than riding, and that it was much easier and more profitable to lose a race than to win one. Either way, the number four horse in the first race and the number seven horse in the second race, both prohibitive longshots, finished first in their runs that day at Mare-Do-Well, yielding a Daily Double payout of $978.32 on a $2 wager. Lessa bet it ten times. The favorites in each race finished second, appearing to make valiant efforts that fell just short.

When the winning numbers and payouts were announced over the public address system, Lessa's knees buckled and she became woozy. She was a strong woman with a sturdy constitution, but this was a new sensation for her, and it caught her utterly off guard. She was holding ten tickets worth nearly $10,000 in total.

Gus was standing nearby, ripping up a stack of losing tickets, when he noticed his sister wobbling. He got to her just as she was regaining her balance and saw she was holding a wad of winning Daily Double tickets. He grabbed for his heart and fell to the ground flat on his back, gyrated a little, then laid completely still. Lessa knew something bad was happening. She screamed for help. Angelo was the closest to them – he was never too far from someone else's winning hand; he could sniff a cut from a mile away. He knelt beside Gus. Lessa let go of her tickets as she clutched Gus with both hands and tried to shake him alert. The tickets were on the floor right where Angelo was kneeling. He swept up the tickets as security personnel and medics were arriving at the scene and walked away casually amid the commotion.

Lessa rode in the ambulance with Gus as it sped to the nearby hospital in Canandaigua, but he was dead even before they got him on the gurney. According to the records he died of a massive heart attack, or atherosclerosis, a coronary artery disease. Doctors told the family that the two eggs and bacon he ate every single morning and the two packs of non-filter Pall Malls he smoked every day for as far back as anybody could remember, had lined his arteries with a layer of plaque so thick that his blood could not flow sufficiently through his circulatory system. His heart just stopped.

That was the official cause of death. Lessa had her own unofficial theory that she believed to be true beyond a shadow of a doubt. The shock of seeing ten winning Daily Double tickets in one place at one time is what stopped Gus's heart cold. Even though the tickets weren't his, they had the same fatal effect.

At the wake, Lessa asked Angelo for her tickets. She was confrontational, clearly upset that he had the balls to take the tickets in the first place, especially under the direst of circumstances.

Angelo tried to mollify her. "I have the cash. The tickets were on the floor, so I picked them up and cashed them for you. I figured they would get lost or taken by someone else. I have the money in the car. I'll go get it."

"No," Lessa said. "Not here. Bring it to the restaurant tomorrow after the funeral. I don't want nobody to know."

Gus's funeral at Saint Thomas Aquinas church and the interment at Saint Patrick's Cemetery were followed by a traditional post funeral Italian luncheon in the restaurant for family, close friends, a couple dozen regulars from the Mare-Do-Well Racetrack and the usual band of blue hairs who attended every funeral at Saint Thomas, regardless of who died, just because it gave them another reason to go to church. In all, about seventy-five people showed up to bid a final farewell to Gus and gorge themselves on the most popular foods on Morelli's menu, as well as a few specialties that never made it to print. There was the requisite chicken soup – a silky layer of grease floating on top of a salty yellow broth with swirling chunks of yesterday's roasted chicken and, of course, the ubiquitous homemade noodles, these particular ones cut in perfect quarter-inch squares. There were huge bowls of rigatoni smothered in dark red tomato sauce; large serving platters piled with a variety of meats, called Ragu – hot and sweet pork sausage, meatballs, braciola and hunks of veal and pork. There was a table with a commercial coffee maker and assorted pastries, Italian cookies called ciambelles made with wine, and cheesecakes. There were a few bottles of Anisette, Sambuca and some other liqueurs that paired well with the pastries and coffee.

While most of the mourners were stuffing their faces, Angelo approached Lessa and handed her an envelope. It was too thick to hold just a mass card, but it had that general appearance, so the exchange did not draw attention. Lessa went into the small closet in the hallway off the back room, where the safe was kept, and opened the envelope. The envelope did in fact hold a mass card, along with fifty $100 bills totaling $5,000. Lessa was livid. The winnings from the ten Daily Double tickets should have been closer to $10,000. She stuffed the cash back into the envelope and slid it under the safe. Lessa headed back to the luncheon with a full head of steam to confront Angelo, but somewhere along the way thought better of creating a scene in front of all the guests. Her and Angelo were the only ones who knew about the tickets, and she wanted to keep it that way.

The large bowls and plates of food were nearly empty. There were no clean coffee cups left on the dessert table and the mounds of pastries had been reduced to crumbs and sugary dust. Every ashtray on every table was filled with cigarette butts, half of them with red lipstick rimming the filters. The white tablecloths were stained with wine and tomato sauce and littered with spent toothpicks. A thick, yellow cloud of smoke wafted near the ceiling as people began filing out of the restaurant through the main dining room door. The regular crew of Morelli's waitresses who attended the services and the luncheon stayed behind to clear the tables before the restaurant closed for the remainder of the day. Early the next morning the cleaning crew would come in to sweep and polish the floors and get the restaurant ready to open for business.

Lessa was waiting near the door, ostensibly to thank people for their prayers and well wishes as they left the restaurant, but her only interest was making sure Angelo didn't leave before she got her money. As he leaned over to kiss her on the cheek, she whispered in his ear that they should talk, and pulled him off to the side by his arm. She was not dainty about it.

"Where's my money?" she demanded.

"It's in the envelope? Didn't you look in the envelope?"

"The rest of it? Where's the rest of it? Where's the rest of the money?"

Angelo was several inches taller than Lessa, so she had to tilt her head at a steep angle to look him in his eyes. He could see that her nostrils were flared and couldn't help feeling a little nervous, even though he was prepared to stand his ground.

"There were five tickets on the floor, and you have every dime of the payout," Angelo said, a tremulous smile crossing his face. "I didn't even take a cut, and you won't ever pay a penny on that money. Gus was down. I was looking out for you."

Angelo made a big mistake. He should have stopped at "five tickets." He might have convinced Lessa of that, and that in the rush at the scene he did not see any other tickets. Maybe they were laying under Gus's dead body, and no one saw them until he was lifted onto the gurney. Possibly someone else saw them and cashed in, or no one saw the tickets and they were swept up and discarded with the day's rubbish. Any of those scenarios were plausible enough for Lessa to accept, or at least cast a rational doubt. But the part about Angelo "looking out" for Lessa, for anyone but himself, she knew was pure nonsense.

125

Lessa called Angelo a liar. "A fucking liar." She threatened to kill him if he didn't come up with the rest of the money. Her face was red; beads of sweat formed on her forehead. She shoved both her hands into his chest hard enough for him to lose his balance and stumble backwards a couple of steps. "You're a fucking liar and a fucking thief!" she said again. "I want my money."

Angelo was running hot himself by now. He didn't like being called a liar or a thief and he sure as hell didn't like being pushed around by a woman.

"You got everything you're gonna get, and that's more than you deserve," he shot back. "Be grateful you got anything you bitch. You're gonna kill me? How you gonna do that? You gonna poison me with your greasy fucking soup? I gotta better idea. Why don't you dig Gus up? You think *I'm* a thief? He probably stuffed the other five tickets up his ass before he croaked. So go fuck yourself. And the next time you get a fucking tip, you better come to me in the first place."

Right in the middle of his abusive rant, Angelo made another mistake.

"The other five tickets?" Lessa questioned. "I never said how many tickets there were. How'd you know there were five more tickets? I want my money!"

"You got your money," Angelo snarled. "Be grateful. You're not getting a penny more and there ain't a damn thing you can do about it." He walked away, leaving the red-faced Lessa clenching her fists.

Most of the family disliked Angelo for various reasons. For the way he talked to Lessa, for the way he came into the restaurant through the back door and filled a plate of whatever food he wanted right from the stovetop. He would even open the oven door to make a withdrawal when he smelled something to his liking. He always left his dirty dish wherever he took his last mouthful. Never said "thank you" or gave a compliment. He never paid for anything, never even offered to pay, yet he never did anything for anybody without expecting payment. Like his vig for running bets to the track, and his cuts on winning tickets. His brother-in-law plowed Morelli's parking lot when it snowed, but it was always Angelo who collected payment, in cash. In the beginning Gus would ask for a bill, only to have Angelo snipe, "What the Christ you need a bill for? I told you he's giving you a goddamn deal. If he puts it in writing he's gotta report it, then everybody will want the same deal." That was total bullshit, of course. Angelo was keeping a cut of the plowing money, even though he never moved a single flake of snow, but Gus figured he was still getting a good price, so he paid the piper. Gus suspected Angelo of overcharging for the cigarettes and cigars he sold to the restaurant, but because he received a discount for paying cash, and occasionally found a few extra cartons of his Pall Mall non-filters behind the bar, he didn't squawk.

CHAPTER SIXTEEN

Cheeseburgers and Chow Mein

The recession of the mid 1970s took a toll on the town and on the restaurant. Lessa had taken over most of Gus's responsibilities for the bar and general management of the business, in addition to her seventy hours a week in the kitchen. Sofia continued to hire and pay the help and entertain the guests who came to visit in the back room. She also put in a full week of work behind the stove. Lessa was the one who opened the kitchen early in the morning, and Sofia was the one who shut it down at night. Amazingly, given the stressful and contentious nature of family businesses, particularly the restaurant trade, the women rarely exchanged harsh words. There was a genetic ebb and flow between the two sisters.

This certain recession would be remembered uniquely as a period of economic stagnation, or "stagflation," where high unemployment and high inflation met head on. Lessa and Sofia didn't understand the cause, but they felt the effect – business was slow. There was an oil crisis which led to high gas prices and gas rationing. People were not about to use up their gas allotments to drive to the other side of town to spend their deflated dollars in an Italian restaurant. They didn't have to. Every major fast-food chain had now opened on the road in and out of Geneva to capitalize on the shrinking discretionary dollar. Hamburgers, pizza, fish & chips, tacos, fried chicken, all-you-can-eat Chinese buffets. The highway had become an international smorgasbord of inexpensive belly fillers that people ate while sitting in Naugahyde-covered booths or took home directly from drive-thru windows. The supermarkets in town started selling ready-to-eat foods like meatloaf and mashed potatoes, macaroni & cheese, hot soups and all the makings for a take-out salad. People could use the same amount of gasoline to get a week's worth of groceries and that night's dinner in a single trip to a single building. The next day they could warm leftovers in the latest kitchen contraption – the microwave oven.

On top of all that, the country had a President who resigned only to save himself from impeachment, and any way you sliced it, an overthrown President was just as bad for America's collective psyche as an assassinated one. People just didn't feel like going to a restaurant for a thick square of authentic lasagna and a bottle of Chianti. They were more secure hunkering down in front of their TVs with a double cheeseburger and a large fountain drink. And, to be sure, Walter Cronkite.

The U.S. metal industry was under attack by newly industrialized countries seeking to sell steel to American factories. The United Can Company, a fixture in the same part of town as Morelli's for as long as anyone knew, was shuttered, leaving hundreds of workers without jobs. In the summer before Nick left for college, he earned some pocket money by opening Morelli's bar until the regular bartenders showed up from their day jobs. He would serve highballs to the United Can employees who came in before they headed home for dinner. He did not know them by name, but he could always pick a United Can worker out in a crowd. They all wore white shirts – short sleeves in the summer, long in the winter – with dark neck ties and a pen or pencil, or both, in their shirt pockets. They wore glasses and used hair tonic to crease their shiny ducktails. As they filed in and out of the bar it was like watching an episode of The Twilight Zone, the black and white TV series. In this episode, all the clones had arrived from another planet and were posing as white-collar workers to observe strange earthling cultures. They looked the same, dressed the same and had the same mannerisms. They smoked cigarettes, on average one-and-a-half per drink. Not a single one of them would leave without dropping a couple of quarters on the bar for Nick to sweep away. Proper tipping of bartenders must have been something they picked up while researching human customs before they journeyed to earth. More than a few would also leave a sip or two of their highballs before they walked out of the bar, which Nick graciously consumed along with the loose change. Friday was his best day. They stayed longer, drank more, and left three quarters or, sometimes, a dollar bill; enough to comfortably get Nick through the weekend, especially since he already had his buzz on by the time he left for the night. They stopped coming in when "The Can" closed.

A considerable textile mill on Eisenhour Road between Morelli's end of town and the New York State Thruway closed soon after the United Can Company, also leaving many families without a working head of household, families that had been regulars at Morelli's on Friday and Saturday nights for many years.

Seneca Lake, the centerpiece of Geneva and home to the annual Fishing Derby every Spring, suffered from industrial pollutants discharged by factories on the south end as well as from the Roosevelt Naval Base, which housed a Warfare Research Center that developed and tested undersea weapon systems on the east side of the lake. When the trout went away so did the fishermen. The beaches closed. There was no boating business for the marinas. Fishermen and boaters had dined often at Morelli's.

To top it all off, Rockers Park, a minor league baseball stadium that opened in 1958 and over the years was home to future stars like Pete Rose, Tony Perez, Bill Madlock and Cesar Tovar, and in 1972 was the site of the first professional baseball game umpired by a woman, lost its major league affiliation with the Washington Senators and subsequently lost its star power. The once pristine, three thousand-seat stadium had deteriorated and was reduced to hosting garish carnivals and flea markets.

By the time the recession hit full force, Morelli's was in the third year of high interest debt that the family had taken on to expand and update the restaurant when the business was booming. A severe winter storm that clobbered the area in the middle of the construction added an unforeseen twenty percent to the construction budget. When the dust cleared, the restaurant could seat more guests in a larger dining room, prepare food faster and more efficiently on modern kitchen equipment, and keep perishable stock at just the right temperatures in spacious new coolers and freezers. The owners even launched a catering service and purchased two new delivery vans upfitted with ovens and coolers so they could reach more people in more places. Good ideas. Bad timing. Ghastly luck.

The recession was the first in a flurry of blows. The 1974 United Farm Workers strike left California vegetable fields unattended. The limited availability and soaring produce prices had Lessa scrambling to sub out the main ingredient in the restaurant's signature dinner salad – iceberg lettuce. Nick was driving now, and at about one in the afternoon every couple of days during summer he would toss a few empty bushel baskets in the trunk of his mother's Chevy and take Lessa to a farm on the old Canandaigua Road, where they picked enough fresh dandelions to fill all the baskets. Lessa would bend over at her hips and pluck the rosettes from the soft, loose soil and then shake the dirt from the roots before dropping them in a basket. Nick was instructed to pick only the greens with the biggest, thinnest, brightest leaves because they were less bitter. When she got back to the restaurant she washed the dandelions in a vigorous spray of cold water, chopped off the white roots and tossed the leaves in a large metal bowl with radish slices and black olives, drenched the salad mix in oil and vinegar and bombarded it with salt and pepper. The taste of dandelion was slightly bitter and more flavorful than iceberg lettuce.

The customers devoured the new dinner salad. If their meal didn't come with a side salad, they ordered it separately. Lessa never charged; she was just happy that her plan to replace the iceberg worked out. So she panicked on the afternoon when her and Nick pulled up to the farm to find a fleet of police cars parked along the road with their lights spinning obnoxiously from blue to red. Officers and Troopers were traipsing through the muddy dandelion field looking for clues. Earlier that morning the farmer found Angelo Nunziato, the cigarette salesman, in his Lincoln Mark IV with a six-inch carpenter's nail driven deep into his forehead. The car was in a ditch on the west end of the field, the Canandaigua side. Angelo was likely coming home from the racetrack. On the seat beside him was that day's "Tip Sheet."

The murder went unsolved. There were no witnesses. The police questioned Lessa, briefly, because she was the only person harvesting the dandelion field in recent days and was a known acquaintance of the victim. She told them she had not seen or heard from Angelo since Gus's funeral. She did not mention, however, that she put a pox on him the very same day Gus was buried, nor did she reveal the reason for the curse. They showed Nick the body and asked if he knew the dead man, but lost interest in his testimony as soon as he puked on the corpse. Angelo's flesh had puckered around the inserted spike and Nick saw a clump of his brain – a pinkish fluffy substance – peering out from the hole in his head. A thin stream of blood had run from the wound down his nose and over his upper lip.

The police found the dead body with no wallet, no money and no jewelry, so they figured he made a score at the track that day and someone followed him, forced him to pull off the road, robbed and killed him. Considering the macabre cause of death and its apparent forethought, police further deduced that the killer must have known Angelo for some time and was not very fond of him to begin with. He was probably just waiting for a good time to nail him. Generally, Angelo was known as an avaricious prick who had enemies near and far.

There were no tears shed for Angelo at Morelli's, but that's not to say the business was unaffected. The restaurant got a new tobacco salesman – a tight ass company man who did everything by the book, and on the books. Invoices. Audits. Alcohol and tobacco filings. Sales tax. There were no more free cartons of cigarettes stashed behind the bar.

Not long after the lettuce crisis of '74, Christian died. He died too young, although he looked much older than his years. The party line said it was cancer, presumably from smoking and drinking, both of which he did right up to his final hours. Non-filters and Dewar's neat. But he was never treated for cancer that anyone knew about. The oncology hospital was in Rochester, about forty miles west of Geneva. The hospital in Geneva didn't have an oncology department. No matter. Christian never checked into any hospital. He died on a sofa in a single room in a dilapidated boarding house on Lewis Street that was home to mostly disabled war veterans. Christian served briefly in the U.S. Navy in his early twenties before being honorably discharged. He moved out of the restaurant and into the boarding house when his illness became apparent. It was not like Christian, a proud and self-reliant person, to depend on others for his health care. When attendants found his lifeless body, he was covered up with a homemade quilt from one of the bedrooms above the restaurant. The quilt smelled like mothballs. To Christian it must have been a comforting, familiar scent. He weighed around a hundred pounds at the time, although in his best days he never weighed more than one-forty or one-fifty. What little hair he had left before he died was white and the skin on his face drooped. His eyes were swollen shut and he could barely talk because his mouth was coated with cold sores. He had only a couple of teeth; most had fallen out by their roots. His face was puckered, his cheekbones pronounced.

Lessa sat beside Christian for most of his last two days. Their relationship over the years was fractious but loving. She was grateful for all the ways he would help around the restaurant and bar. She relied on him to keep track of the inventory in the walk-in refrigerator and the freezers, making sure they never ran short on steaks or fish. He routinely checked the basement for giant cans of tomatoes. Whenever Christian booked a large party over the phone he was cordial and precise – time, head count, menu, seating preference – and he stressed, in a pleasant but serious tone, that the party be prompt. If the restaurant needed an extra dishwasher, it was Christian. If a bartender called in sick, Christian filled in. He had his regular nights behind the stove and he never missed a shift. He was also great with the children in the family – Lessa's grandchildren. He cut their hair and made sure it was stylish, according to what he deemed to be stylish. Dennis and Nick, the oldest of the grandchildren, were his favorites. When he ran errands for the restaurant, he would always take one or both along for the ride, and if they wanted ice cream he would treat at the Dairy Queen. He took them shopping for clothes; not straight leg Wrangler jeans and flannel shirts like all the other boys were wearing, but bell bottoms and hip huggers, wide leather belts, V-neck sweaters. He bought them underwear, though they always had plenty. Edie bought Dennis and Nick underwear on all gift occasions – birthdays, Christmas. She even put a three-pack of white BVDs in their Easter baskets every year. (One year, Dennis ripped open his three-pack and mashed a chocolate bunny into one of the undies. "Hey Ma, looks like you bought me used underwear," he said. "I ain't wearing these." Edie removed the BVDs from the basket and emptied all the treats in the garbage.) Christian needed no such occasion to buy them underwear. It could be a Tuesday in the middle of summer. "Here. Try them on. Make sure they fit," he would say. Underwear always fit, and who cared if they didn't? Dennis and Nick never tried them on, despite Christian's urging.

It was what Christian did after he left Morelli's that troubled Lessa, even though she was never sure what that was. He would leave late in the evening, usually after the restaurant closed, even on nights when he wasn't working. On most nights, or early mornings, she could hear him staggering into his bedroom. He was not typically alone.

The time Lessa spent with Christian on his final day was mostly quiet. He couldn't talk, and she didn't know what to say, so it worked out. She had some ideas for specials on the weekend's menu that might have interested him in other times – he always wanted to know what Lessa was cooking up – but it didn't feel right to talk about food with a man who had no appetite. A couple of times he struggled to open his eyes and Lessa could see through narrow slits the white part of his eyeball coated with a milky membrane. She could see a contorted grin form on his face for a second. He put his hand on top of hers and in a raspy, barely audible voice, he said good-bye. It was time for both of them to leave.

It was never publicly certain how Christian ended up in Geneva. One suggestion had him run out of his home and business in Hollywood, California, where he was a hairdresser deluxe, maybe not to the stars but certainly to a top rung of society's ladder. Rumors suggested drugs, and debt. He was Lessa Donato's godchild and he knew he always had a home with her, no questions asked. Regardless of how it came to be, he was living in a suburban bumfuck, by his standards, and he never matriculated. He never adapted. He figured Geneva should rise to him. It did not. He was unpretentious about being pretentious. He lived life his way, wherever he happened to be living at the time.

Christian's death was a blow to the restaurant on several counts. He tended bar, took inventory, ran errands. He was a very popular hairdresser in the beauty shop above the restaurant. He was an excellent cook. His real talent was at the broiler. His steaks and chops were always perfect. He had no fear of the thick, rolling flames coming off the top of the broiler as he plucked and turned his seared sirloins and fillets with a long steel fork. He never wore oven mitts and had the burn scars on the top of his right hand as evidence. Christian could work late into any night of the week since his social life didn't start until around midnight, after he shaved, showered and dressed like he had a hot date, although nobody remembered him ever having a formal date for any event. During the days he woke around two in the afternoon and cut blue hairs for a couple hours. In the late afternoon he changed into a clean white tee shirt, white pants, a white apron and took his place behind the stove. When he wasn't cooking, he was tending bar. Until midnight he was the property of Morelli's Restaurant. After that he was up for anything.

Even those who viewed Christian with a jaundiced eye tolerated him because he worked hard for the family business. Most people have a millisecond in their brains between thought and speech. Christian had no such filter. If he didn't like your clothes or your hair or the way you talked, he told you. Then he told you how to fix what he didn't like. Even if he liked you, he condescended to you. He was naturally flamboyant, and in a working-class town like Geneva, flamboyance generally rubbed people the wrong way. He wore neatly pressed bell bottom pants and platform shoes. His shirts were silky and loud with wide collars unbuttoned enough to show off the gold chain around his neck. His thick, black, curly hair was always freshly trimmed and neatly coiffed around his rakishly handsome face. He could have been a movie star. Dennis and Nick kept waiting for him to bring home a beautiful girl for them to ogle, like one of the girls on the posters in Vinny's bedroom, but he never did. They figured there were no girls in Geneva good enough for Christian.

Lessa had to recruit two cooks to make up for the hours that Christian put in. One came from another restaurant where he was a short order cook. He was adequate. The other was a recent graduate of a culinary college who was looking for a start. His first night on the job he showed up wearing a toque and white chef's coat. He didn't last long. The next person she hired might have worked out had one of the waitresses, who was dating a parole officer at the time, not discovered he was recently released from prison after serving a term for arson. Lessa figured that one ex-con under her roof was sufficient.

Over the next couple of years Lessa Donato and her family went through all the trials and tribulations of running a restaurant amid dramatic shifts in the social and economic landscapes of a small town on a big lake. Besides the external influences, the cultural fabric of the family itself was changing. Sustaining the family business was not as important to the later generations as college, travel, normal jobs in law, medicine, sales, banking. Moreover, they simply did not want to work as hard as the generations before them.

The restaurant was running out of cooks. The ones that remained loyal to the business were working more days and longer hours, even though traffic in the restaurant was still down from where it was before the renovations and recession. The economy was improving a bit, but by now people were accustomed to tightening their belts. Their way of life had changed, probably for good. They had other options. The recession hit the restaurant's end of Geneva harder than the rest of the town. All the new retail businesses and food chains were opened clear on the other side of Geneva. It was a more vibrant area. More inviting. More to do. There was a giant Walmart. By comparison, the railroad tracks near the restaurant were now uncontrollably overgrown with colorless, thorny weeds. The old train station, once a solid, red brick bastion that brought a historic nobility to the neighborhood, was ramshackle and unsightly. It was the first thing people saw when they pulled into Morelli's parking lot.

The only difference inside the kitchen at Morelli's were the shiny new appliances that were part of the overhaul. The food was the same – fresh, homemade, authentic, creative, cooked perfectly, presented plainly but pleasingly. Regardless of who was behind the stove,

Lessa was in control of the kitchen. Every dish had to be perfect before it went on a tray. She made her sauce, or gravy, with whole and crushed tomatoes and various herbs cooked on a low fire and simmered for hours so that the meats would absorb the flavor of the sauce, and vice versa. The meatballs would be moist, the chunks of pork tender and juicy. The braciola would not have to be sliced with a knife; it would pull apart with a fork. She always made just enough sauce to last for one night, even though most of the people walked in without reservations, so she never knew in advance how many meals she would serve during a shift. Morelli's never turned away a customer, even on the nights when it was busiest. The next day she would start a new caldron of sauce with the same ingredients. And she always let the sauce simmer.

Lessa never roasted garlic, even when every boiler-plate Italian restaurant chain crowding America's malls and strip centers started roasting garlic as a sensory aid to mask fast sauce and boxed noodles under the guise of nouveau cuisine. Lessa did garlic one way and one way only – sliced transparently thin and fried in olive oil, maybe with some hot pepper. It was the base for her tomato sauce and sautéed greens, although it was present in many other dishes. One of her specialties and a favorite on the menu was "greens & beans," sautéed greens, usually rapini – or broccoli rabe – with white cannellini beans fried with the garlic and oil and a sprig of fresh sage. Sometimes she would throw in a piece of a hot pepper and some crumbled sausage, depending on her mood. The enticing fragrance of garlic frying in oil permeated every room in the giant house. A family favorite was thick slices of bologna fried in oil and garlic, with a little vinegar in the pan so the meat would caramelize and wouldn't taste gamey. Fried bologna between two slices of plain white bread with plain yellow mustard. Sweet Jesus that was good. Eventually fried bologna wound up as an appetizer on the menu at Morelli's.

Lessa, and Morelli's, were old school all the way. Macaroni in any shape was always homemade. Ravioli and Manicotti were stuffed by hand, with ricotta cheese, not meat. Lessa just didn't believe in meat ravioli. It was over the edge. Once, she fried a steak with oil, garlic, fresh mushrooms, and a hot pepper and, on a whim, plopped a mound of plain spaghetti on top of the steak and poured the dark, shiny pan drippings over the entire plate. She was eating it in the back room when someone came in and asked, "What is that? Black spaghetti? It smells amazing."

"Black Spaghetti with Steak & Mushrooms" was handwritten under "Specials" on the menu the following Saturday night. The next week it was "Black Spaghetti with Pork Chop & Hot Peppers." Before long customers just ordered "Black Spaghetti à la Morelli," and the kitchen would send it out with whatever cut of meat was on hand.

Even the toast Lessa made for breakfast was not standard issue Wonder White Bread. It was thick slices of crusty Italian bread toasted under the broiler then schmeared with warm, salty butter. The eggs were never scrambled or poached or turned over in any way; they were fried sunny side up in a frothy puddle of butter and olive oil.

Once a week she made submarine sandwiches – not hoagies or heroes or grinders like the pizza parlors were selling. Lessa's "sub" started with a half loaf of fresh Italian bread and a thick sheath of shredded iceberg lettuce, which for some reason complemented the other ingredients in the sandwich much better than whole leaf lettuce or

Romaine. There were layers of ham, salami, capicola and mortadella, all neatly and evenly sliced on a commercial grade Hobart meat slicer; cold, freshly sliced tomatoes; round provolone cheese slices – sharp provolone so that it would not be overwhelmed by all the cured Italian meats; and a combination of hot and sweet peppers. On the top piece of bread she ran a stream of oil and vinegar and sprinkled garlic powder on that. This was a submarine, the perfect name for the perfect sandwich. A life-long comfort food right up there with spaghetti and meatballs and chicken cacciatore.

One day, also on a whim, Lessa mashed together a couple of cold meatballs, sprinkled in some grated parmesan, and spooned the resulting mush between two thin slices of Italian bread. She ignored the few strands of spaghetti that clung to the meatballs as she pulled them from the bucket of sauce, wrapped the sandwiches in foil, placed them in wrinkled brown paper bags and sent her grandkids off to Saint Thomas Aquinas Elementary with their lunch. Nick was sitting with the usual cast of characters at lunch that day – Artie Bolger, Billy Talucci, Marty Scher, Johnny DiPadova, Jeff Feola, Marc Snyderman and Leo Lusco – when sure enough the first bite of his sandwich left a rogue noodle dangling down his chin just long enough for his friends to see him slurp it into his mouth. All hell broke loose. "Nicky's eating a macaroni sandwich," Leo yelled to the entire lunch crowd. The boys laughed. The girls made squeamish noises as if Nick were sucking down a night crawler. The haranguing was of no concern to him. While the other kids were choking down their bologna or PBJ or tuna or egg salad sandwiches, or whatever else their harried moms slapped together that morning between sips of coffee, he was feasting on the delicacy that was a homemade meatball sandwich assembled thoughtfully by his dear Grandma Lessa. A stray noodle was merely a bonus.

Lessa was to cooking what Irving Berlin was to music. He could not read or write a single note, yet he authored some of the most beloved show tunes of all time, including White Christmas, another favorite on the old jukebox in the Morelli's bar during the winter holidays. Lessa intuitively created all her own dishes; she didn't work from recipes, she authored them. She didn't mimic foods she tried in other restaurants, not that she had occasion to patronize other restaurants as a routine practice. She didn't plan things out in advance or have concoctions come to her in her sleep. Her cooking was instinctive. Spontaneous. Not derivative. It was transcendent. And she made sure it was always affordable for the working class that frequented her restaurant. She refused to raise prices even after the restaurant began accepting credit cards and had to pay service fees for that privilege. The plastic payments also meant official receipts, which meant official sales taxes, which meant more formal accounting oversight. Formal accounting – formal anything – was never standard operating procedure at Morelli's. To be fair, formal accounting was not the norm at most small, family-owned businesses at the time.

CHAPTER SEVENTEEN
Checking Out, Checking In

When Dominic DiLorenzo died in 1990 it was of little consequence to the family business as such – the finicky old jukebox in the bar that accepted only red polished quarters had been replaced a couple years earlier with a Wurlitzer 1015 that used a compact-disc technology developed by a Japanese company. He was too feeble to do any handywork around the house or tend to Lessa's garden, which he was apt to do once she put in a few hot pepper plants. But the emotional toll his passing took on Lessa was far more severe than any of the business setbacks she had to endure, including the suspension of the restaurant's liquor license in the 1960s, the lettuce price hike in 1974 and, most recently, the great tomato shortage in 1985 caused by unseasonably cold weather in Florida in January, February and

March of that same year. Wholesale prices for tomatoes skyrocketed from around $7 per twenty-five-pound box to $30. Fortunately for the restaurant, Lessa had a bumper crop of tomatoes in her backyard garden that season, the kind of tomatoes you could wipe clean on your tee shirt and bite into. Homegrown heirloom tomatoes, not hard and unscented like supermarket tomatoes that looked as though they were painted red and smelled like insect repellent. Lessa's tomatoes were aromatic. Fragrant. Their vines were thick, green, and healthy. The tomatoes were softer. They were deep red. And they had an organic sweetness, natural, not tangy. She had to charge more for her tomatoes because they were in such short supply. It was one of the few times she raised the price of a staple, and it was a decision she agonized over even though it was only by a few cents. Her customers complained about the higher prices, but they asked for the homegrown tomatoes in their salads and antipastos anyway. As soon as the restaurant was again able to procure tomatoes at a reasonable cost, she immediately lowered the prices on salads, antipastos and other dishes that featured "fresh" tomatoes. Customers continued to ask for the homegrown variety.

Lessa walked around in a stupor for weeks after Dominic died. She mourned for a much longer time than she did after Gus passed away. When Gus died, she made the funeral arrangements, planned the luncheon, and made a list of his work responsibilities that she and her sister Sofia would have to account for now that he was gone. Except for those few minutes at the track when he died in her arms, Lessa seemed to hardly mourn at all. In fact, Gus's death was more like part of the business; a hitch that needed her consideration.

Lessa handled all the funeral arrangements for Dominic in meticulous fashion, yet she found no closure in the process. She roamed the giant house for the next several days and nights doing mostly light housekeeping. She made the sauce every morning; she had been doing it for so long that she could do it flawlessly without attentiveness. Her family, the ones closest to her, feared that she was over medicating. When they decided she was more of a hazard than a help in the kitchen, they convinced her to visit her doctor. The diagnosis was clinical depression and the doctor urged her to check into the psychiatric hospital on the other side of the lake. Astonishingly, Lessa agreed without contention. She was tired. Uninspired. The possibility existed that after running the restaurant and reigning as the matriarch of a large and ever growing family; after burying a stillborn baby, her father and mother, her brothers Rocco and Gus, her godson Christian, and now a man that had been part of her family since before she was born; after her eldest daughter was physically and emotionally crippled in a fiery car crash hundreds of miles away from the comfort of her arms, Lessa may have simply given up. The family's concern was not so much that she readily agreed to enter such a facility, but that she might not agree to leave it as eagerly. Edie and Lucky drove their mother to the hospital when it was time. The sisters cried quietly for most of the trip. Lessa was silent. When they pulled up to the front door of the stately Victorian style building, Edie turned off the engine and retrieved her mother's tattered, timeworn suitcase from the trunk. As she set the bag down beside the three of them at the admission desk in the lobby, Lucky looked at it and said, "Jesus Christ Ma. When you gonna get some new luggage?"

"Where my gonna go Lucky?" a despondent Lessa replied.

By the time Lessa left the "nut house" – that's how the family referred to the hospital, in part because they were insensitive assholes and in part because they knew if they didn't joke about it they'd be overcome with the guilt that they all had something to do with putting her there – the country was in the final leg of another recession characterized by sluggish employment and inadequate economic expansion that the sitting U.S. President blamed on the previous U.S. President.

Edie Donato Poole died in 1994, a week before Thanksgiving. She had been sick for many years – not just because of the accident in 1955 but also because of all the maladies that followed. Before she was fifty, she was diagnosed with degenerative heart failure, Type 1 Diabetes, and ulcers. There were many aspects of her life that dumbfounded her closest relatives and friends for as long as they knew her. Her spirit, or mood, around the Thanksgiving holiday was one of the most astounding. The horrendous car crash that crippled her forever, crippled her physically and emotionally, that probably ended her marriage, occurred on a Thanksgiving Day. Yet, rather than sad ruminations, she greeted this anniversary with vim and vigor. Some thought her joy was all about festive family gatherings, decorations, turkey with stuffing and all the trimmings, a day off from work, department store discounts. Others concluded that her bliss had little or nothing to do with seasonal rituals and general good tidings. Rather, she cherished Thanksgiving Day because on this day, instead of losing three children, she was blessed to share a lifetime with them.

The summer before Edie died, she took a vacation with her family to the ocean. She spent a lot of time with her grandchildren. All her kids had at least one of their own. She played poker and bingo. She grew up in a gambling environment and never got it out of her system. She loved to play cards, but she was not very good at it.

Edie died in her sleep. She was covered up, wearing her glasses. The TV was on, tuned to some "whodunnit" serial, her unequivocal favorite genre. She seemed peaceful and comfortable. For forty years, ever since the accident in Ohio, Edie woke up every morning and limped through the day. She lived with more sickness and pain than she let on. She had good days, and people would rarely know about her bad days because through them all she never lost her spirit. It wasn't always her physical disabilities that she had to battle. Edie also lived with the tremendous emotional burden that as much as she was able to do for her children, it wasn't enough. She worried that her physical limitations kept her from being a normal mom, from doing normal mom things with her children. Her kids were pampered and punished. They were pampered more than they deserved.

The wake for Edie Donato Poole at Luhmann's Funeral Home drew such a large crowd that the Geneva Police Department had to assign four squad cars just to handle the traffic. The viewing line reached the front sidewalk near the curb, and it did not move quickly. Hundreds of people came to pay their respects.

Mary Lou Malloy was there. She gently tugged at Nick's elbow while he was talking with another mourner. "I'm so sorry about your mom, Nicky. She was wonderful. She was so kind to me and my father." Her voice was soft and sad. There were tears in her eyes. But she was every bit as sexy as Nick remembered her to be on that Fourth of July in 1968, and he wondered if she was having the same thoughts he was having.

They sat for a while in the back of the room and caught up. They reminisced about the neighborhood, about the gang from Soldier's Playground on North Walnut Street. She asked about his brothers and sister. Naturally, Nick asked about Gordy Vogel, although he was sure she would have purged that dullard from her life when she left Geneva.

"He's doing great," she said. "He's in construction."

"You still hear from him?"

"Every day. We're married."

Nick was dumbstruck. "Oh, that's great," he muttered, doing his best to conceal the jolt. To his utter bewilderment, the one-time girl of his dreams married that soul-sucking neanderthal. She never did become a nurse. She married a construction worker in Florida, and together they had three children – a boy and two girls. Nick quickly did the math in his head. The boy was old enough to have been born while Mary Lou was still a teenager. He was several years older than his two sisters.

A few more minutes of small talk and they kissed goodbye.

That night Nick was having a drink with his cousin Michael and telling him about his conversation with Mary Lou.

"Oh yeah, I saw you talking to her today," Michael said. "She's doing really good." Michael was friendly with some of the Vogels still living in Geneva.

"What do you mean 'doing good?' She married that moron Gordy Vogel, a real hammer head," Nick countered. "He's probably still building sheds. She could have done so much better. She could have married a doctor."

"Where'd you hear that? Gordy's the biggest contractor in central Florida," Michael said. "He's got, like, nine hundred people working for him. He's worth millions. He specializes in medical buildings and places that do radiology. Shit like that. Doctors wish they had his money. I don't think he's working too much anymore though. His boy, Gordy, Jr., pretty much runs the business now. Gordy and Mary Lou mostly just travel. His mother told me they have a home in Palm Springs. Built it himself. They're in Geneva now visiting his mother. I heard she's in the hospital. Did you know he bought her that real big house on Castle Hill Road? Out past the Experiment Station. Remember who used to live there Nicky? Dr. Banka. He was your mother's doctor. His wife Sora used to visit with Aunt Lessa and my mother all the time in the back room."

Nick took a long, thoughtful sip of his drink, digesting the notion of Mary Lou and Gordy living in eternal bliss. Before he put his drink back on the table, he decided that he was happy for Gordy. He turned out to be a much better person than anyone could have expected. If he did knock up Mary Lou when they were teenagers, he didn't hide in a closet. He must have followed her to Florida, married her, took care of her, and provided a great life for his family. He must have always loved her. And she him. Way back when, Mary Lou Malloy saw something in Gordy Vogel that no one else saw. Good for her. Lucky for him.

CHAPTER EIGHTEEN

Batter Up

Edie's death was a blow to the family and to the business. She was the heir apparent to Morelli's kitchen, even though she lacked any real business acumen. Lessa took it hard, but it was as if she were calloused over. She seemed to accept death. In Edie's case, maybe, she thought it was merciful. She did not expect that kind of mercy for herself. She was on so much medication by now she was a liability in the kitchen for any longer than it took to make the sauce in the morning, which she still accomplished in perfunctory fashion.

The restaurant was now being run by an ad hoc committee of family members who combined to take legal and operational ownership from Lessa and Sofia. It was temporary, and they all knew it. They could cook, it was their birthright, after all. They kept things running more out of respect for the legacy of Morelli's than for the passion. The $300,000 debt from the renovations hung over all their heads. They knew it was time to get out. The building and the business were in good enough shape to sell, but could they get out debt-free, albeit with nothing really to show for seven decades of blood, sweat and tomato sauce? The assessed value of the restaurant and building was about half of the amount they owed, and nary an offer came in even at that discounted price tag. Another local restaurateur made a nibble well under the amount needed to lift the family out of its financial hole.

There weren't a lot of options. Bankruptcy would help pay off some of the debt but not the total amount. Many of the vendors were local businesses and longtime friends of the family. No one wanted to short them. It was decided to close the restaurant while every prudent solution was explored, rather than go further into debt. It simply cost more to stay open than receipts would cover.

The entire family – those who were still in the vicinity – pitched in to get the place cleaned up and ready to sell in case that were to happen. No one lived upstairs any longer – all the residents either died or moved out to start their own families. Or just went away with no explanation or known destination. Nick took a week off from his job as a weather forecaster for a Boston TV station to come back to help and stayed in one of the vacant bedrooms upstairs. He wanted to sleep in the house he virtually grew up in one more time before it changed hands. Before he fell asleep each night, he relived with astonishing clarity his life in this grand place. The highs and lows. The laughing, the crying. And, more than he liked to admit, the whining and hissy fits. The comings and goings. He remembered all the people who passed through Morelli's and what they contributed to the culture. He thought about the amazing food.

He could almost smell the sauce simmering and the garlic and oil frying in the kitchen. He could hear the locomotive squealing to a long, slow halt in front of the Lehigh Valley train station.

Nick remembered the cool, damp, musty air in the basement below the bar, and how when he went down there as a kid to carry up the ice he would run his hand along the wall at the bottom of the stairs to feel for the light switch, wondering every time why the idiot who built the place did not put the switch at the top of the stairs. If he didn't feel it right away, he would run back up the stairs to catch his breath, and then start over again. He remembered how the clunking sound of the ice machine always scared him, even as he became intimately familiar with it. He remembered the unevenness of the cement floor as he walked from the bottom of the stairs to the tiny room where the noisy machine was kept.

Lessa was now living with Buster and his family. He converted his den on the first floor of his Tudor style house on Markwell Avenue into a bedroom for his mother, since it was a challenge for her to go up and down stairs. There was a bathroom adjacent to her room which for all intents and purposes was hers exclusively. Her cooking was pretty much limited to quick lunches and after school snacks for Buster's four kids, since Buster's wife, Susan, cooked most of the main meals. Grilled cheese sandwiches were Lessa's specialty now. She used three kinds of cheese, sautéed onions, a couple slices of home-grown tomato and some fresh basil. Nothing about Lessa's cooking was ordinary, ever.

One day, while Nick was cleaning out the basement at Morelli's, he heard his Uncle Buster call from the top of the steps. His call was loud and abrupt, and it scared Nick stiff, which was more than likely Buster's intention. It reminded Nick of all the times when, as a boy, he would be in that dark, dank basement filling ice buckets for the bar wells, and one of the bartenders – an older cousin, an uncle, even an occasional waitress who had no reason whatsoever to seek him out – would yell sharply from the top of the stairs with the sole intention of petrifying him. Nick took a certain melancholic comfort in the thought that this was likely the last time he would be in this dreaded basement and therefore the last time anyone would intentionally or unintentionally scare the holy shit out of him. Buster likely had the same sentiment, that this would be the last opportunity for him to scare Nick senseless. He would miss this more than his nephew.

Buster had driven his mother to Morelli's so that she could go through the last of her belongings in her bedroom. He asked Nick to stay with her, to keep her company and to carry the boxes she packed downstairs. "Probably just some clothes and jewelry," he told Nick. "The Salvation Army will be by later this week to take the furniture. I have to run some errands. I'll be back to get her in a couple of hours. Make sure she doesn't pack more than I can fit in my car."

Lessa Donato lived in this house for most of a century. She raised and presided over a family large enough to fill a high school gymnasium. She ran a business through depressions, recessions, drought, disease, death, allegations, and investigations – like her personal Seven Plagues of Revelation. She cooked millions of meals – half of those for Nick, he figured. There was no way he would ever tell her what she could or could not take with her, despite Buster's instructions. He sat on the edge of her bed as she went through the drawers in her dresser. Considering the circumstances, she moved with surprising alacrity. Then again, she could have just been anxious to get this part of her life over. She pulled a teak wood jewelry box from one of the drawers and held it on her lap while she sat on the bed beside Nick. The first thing she pulled out of the box was her late husband's gold

Gruen watch. Nick could tell it was old and, as she fiddled with it, he saw that the clasp on the chain didn't catch.

"You can have it," she said, and handed it to Nick with no apparent fanfare or pomp. To Nick, the gesture seemed arbitrary; he was the one who happened to be in her room on that day at that time, so he was gifted the watch. Had Buster stayed with her while she packed, he certainly would have been given the watch. Dennis, her first-born grandchild and a more rightful heir to the watch, was now living on Lake Barkley in Western Kentucky. He left school during his senior year to be with his pregnant girlfriend, even though she told him he was not guaranteed to be the father. Her parents sent her to Kentucky to have the baby. Her Uncle John – her father's brother – owned a dude ranch and gave Dennis a job. A year later, the baby's real father, who was also Dennis's best friend in high school, showed up and took his new family to California. By then Dennis had become a valued employee at the dude ranch, so he decided to stay put on Lake Barkley. He loved working with the horses and was the ranch's best trail guide. He had more responsibilities than the head wrangler, although he was paid much less. Dennis, from time to time, even filled in as camp cook, and his barbequed meats received five-star raves from his co-workers and guests.

The teak box also contained one walnut and several envelopes gathered in a rubber band. They were addressed to Attica Prison, Attica, New York, Prisoner No. 289C0441. They came from Josephine Morelli, c/o Morelli's Restaurant, 59 Lehigh Lane, Geneva, New York 14456. Out of curiosity, Nick tried to remove one of the letters from its envelope, but his grandmother snatched it away before he could get a look at its content. Any interest he had at all in the letters was quickly dispatched when he noticed the final item in the box – a baseball card wrapped in clear plastic that had blended in with the letters. Nick was enough of a baseball fan to know that this card was special – a 1910 Honus Wagner. The card was pristine, with crisp white borders and solid, pointy corners. Wagner was posed stoically in his flannel gray baseball jersey with a dark blue collar and "PITTSBURGH" emblazoned across the chest. He was hatless, and his hair was parted perfectly down the middle. The figure was silhouetted against a goldenrod background as vibrant as the day the card was printed. It occurred to Nick that he might have been one of only five, maybe six people who had ever held this card.

"Grandma, where did you get this?" he asked anxiously. "Do you know what this is? Do you know *who* this is?"

Lessa was about as interested in the baseball card as Nick was in the walnut. "Yeah, I know. It's a baseball card. Dominic gave it to me before he died. Told me to hold onto it. Said it would be worth something someday. I don't know why. He got it a long time ago, from his friend Leone. His family used to own the farm on the way to Canandaigua where we picked dandelions. Remember when we used to pick dandelions, Nicky? Dominic used to help on the farm sometimes. Maybe that's when he got the baseball card from Leone. He shoulda got money. But he loved baseball. That must be a Yankee player. The Yankees was his favorite team."

Nick was mesmerized by the baseball card he was still holding in his hand. "It's not a Yankee," he told his grandmother without looking away from Wagner's image.

"Not a Yankee?"

"No. But I think it's worth something. Can I show this to Uncle Buster?"

"I don't care. What could it be worth?" Lessa smirked. "It's not even a Yankee."

It was a T206 Honus Wagner card, one of the most famous and rarest of all his cards, of any baseball card. A reputable memorabilia collector and auctioneer in Cooperstown, New York, home of the Baseball Hall of Fame, authenticated the card as "near mint" because he thought it had been "slightly altered;" that the edges had been trimmed to regain some of its form, and the consequence was that the card's dimensions were off by a fraction of a fraction of an inch from its original size, completely imperceptible to the naked eye. The card was graded nine-and-a-half on a scale of one-to-ten based on its condition. Nonetheless, the card, "as is," was valued at around $450,000. After several family meetings and negotiations with the collector, Buster and Michael sold the card for $50,000 below its assessed value. They were in a hurry to get the cash. The money, after taxes, combined with the sale of the restaurant, was enough to get the family out of debt and even put a few dollars in the bank for Buster, Michael and the other owners, and set up Lessa and Sofia in comfortable apartments in a newly-built assisted living home adjacent to the very hospital where all their children and grandchildren were born.

"Dominic and his goddamn knives," Michael told Buster after the sale. "You know what that card would be worth if he left it alone? Two million. Maybe more."

DiLorenzo did get the Wagner card from Leone, but not in a trade for another card or as payment for farm work. Leone was in fact at home the night of the murder in 1935. He let the fugitive into his house, fed him, packed him some food, and gave him a change of clothes and a flashlight. One day, Leone visited his friend at Attica to thank him for not telling the police of his culpability. Had the truth been told at the time of the investigation, Leone likely would have spent a few years in prison himself, while DiLorenzo's sentence might have been shaved by a few years. He gave DiLorenzo the Wagner card and promised that one day it would be more valuable than any New York Yankee card. Leone died before DiLorenzo was released from prison and was buried on his farm in Phelps. He was penniless.

CHAPTER NINETEEN
Tattered Genes

A couple years after Lessa moved into "the home," Nick began compiling a cookbook of his mother's most popular dishes. The idea came to him after she died, and he found her green steel recipe box in the room she occupied when she visited his family in a suburb of Boston. Her recipes were handwritten on index cards, some of the cards contained notes that brought a certain personality, or history, to the dish. For example, if a recipe were a favorite of someone close to her, she would write the person's name on the card. If she allowed for an ingredient substitution, she noted the potential influences on the resultant dish. Some of the recipes were not to be altered in any way, and in those cases, she emphasized with a heavy pencil, they should be prepared "exactly like this with no exceptions no exclusions no excuses." These untouchables came from cooks who worked in the Morelli's kitchen down through the years, or from people who made homemade desserts for the restaurant to sell. Some came from Edie's friends who had no affiliation with Morelli's. Alongside many of the recipes was scrawled a single two-letter word: "Ma." They were Lessa's dishes.

While Nick was working on the cookbook, he made several trips to Geneva to visit with his grandmother in her apartment. The visits were stretched out over three years because he was busy tracking weather and raising a family and could not concentrate full-time on writing a cookbook. During the earliest stages of the book, Lessa grasped the concept of what he was doing and was very helpful. She spoke with attentive clarity about cooking. What she cooked. How she cooked it. She described the tastes and smells of certain herbs and spices and how they worked with other ingredients in a dish. She was doing a little cooking in her apartment – simple dishes – and sometimes she would make something for Nick. On a few trips he would take his wife and kids and, on those occasions, Lessa would prepare a dessert from Edie's repertoire, like her famous Coconut Cloud Pie, or her Dessert Lasagna. She would tell the kids how people used to come from miles away to have one of their Grandma Edie's desserts. She said her desserts were "world famous."

By the time Nick got to the end of his cookbook project Lessa was well into her eighties and her interest in food was waning. One afternoon, while he was reading her a recipe for Chicken Cacciatore (braised chicken parts on the bone cooked with onions, herbs, tomatoes, bell peppers, wine), Lessa blurted out: "This was my father's favorite dish. He really liked when Mama could make it with rabbit, better than chicken. The guys used to hunt for rabbit. They always made sure Mama got some to use in her cacciatore."

"I never knew your father," Nick said.

"You knew him," Lessa replied in a very calm voice.

"He died when I was just a baby. I have no memory of him."

"That was Joseph. He was married to my mother. He raised me. But he wasn't my father. Not my real father. Not your great grandfather."

Nick was sure his grandmother was confused. It could have been a doolally brought on by the shear boredom of living by herself after decades amid the Morelli's milieu. He tried to straighten her out but was careful not to push too hard. He gently recited the facts as he believed to be true.

"Joseph Morelli was your father. Josephine Morelli was your mother. The restaurant was your family's name. You were born in Italy and came here with your parents when you were a little girl." Nick was sure of the history because in elementary school he had to draw a family tree. He would sit at the kitchen table in his house with his mother and a freshly sharpened pencil. Right at the top of the tree were Joseph and Josephine Morelli, and on the branches below were Lessa Donato and her siblings – Sofia, Gus, and Rocco. On the third row of branches were Edie, Lucky and Buster, then Edie's kids and their cousins. One year, for Christmas, someone gave Lessa and her siblings a portrait of their parents – Joseph and Josephine – made from a photograph that was probably taken at their wedding in Italy because they looked very young and were dressed in formal attire. That portrait hung for years on a wall in the restaurant between the bar and the dining room. You couldn't miss it. The gold plate on the bottom of the frame had the inscription:

Joseph and Josephine Morelli
Founders
Morelli's Restaurant

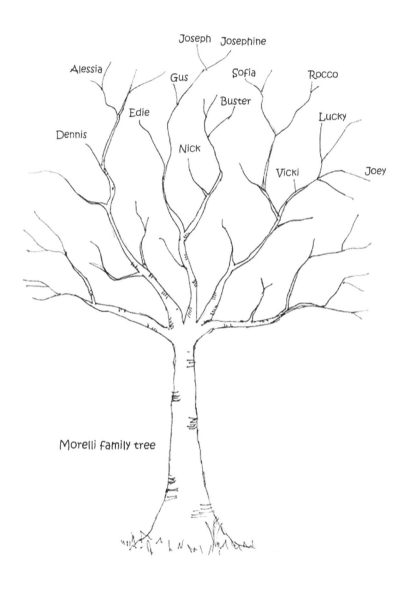

Joseph Josephine
Alessia
Gus
Sofia
Rocco
Buster
Edie
Lucky
Dennis
Nick
Vicki
Joey

Morelli family tree

With all this verification there was no mistake about Lessa's father. There was no doubt about the maternal family tree that Nick and his mother created years before. Who knew what was swirling in Lessa's mind at her advanced age?

She got up from her chair and walked to a chest of drawers in the foyer area of the apartment. From the top drawer she pulled out the same teak jewelry box she showed Nick in her bedroom the day he helped her move out of Morelli's. Nick remembered the box for holding the Honus Wagner baseball card. The only things left in the box were the walnut and the stack of letters addressed from Attica Prison.

"Do you know what these are?" she asked as she lifted the letters from the box. "They're letters from my mother to Dominic. When he was in prison."

That part of her rambling made a certain sense to Nick. They were good friends from their days as young adults in Italy. Dominic was her husband's best friend for most of a lifetime. It wouldn't surprise anybody who knew the three of them that if someone were going to write letters to Dominic DiLorenzo while he was in prison, it would be Josephine. Writing letters, even to a close friend, would have been inconsistent with Joseph's sense of self-importance. He most definitely would never have communicated in any way to a convict. His affiliation with certain figures from New York City already had cast a suspicious cloud over him.

"What do those letters have to do with you and your father?" Nick asked.

"Dominic was my father. My real father."

Nick's immediate thought was that this bizarre claim was attributable to dementia, although Lessa, generally, still had her wits about her.

"Grandma, Dominic was your friend. He came here with your parents. He helped your father build the restaurant. He had his own room upstairs in the house on Lehigh Lane. Remember that?"

"You think I'm crazy, don't you?" Lessa said.

She pulled one of the letters from its envelope and waved it at Nick. "These are all the letters my mother wrote to Dominic when he was in prison. They're in Italian, so I couldn't read them by myself. Just some words and small sentences. My friend, Mary Battaglia, you remember her? She came to the house and made the gnocchi after Cloris Morris died. She read them to me."

Lessa pulled one letter after another and unfolded them, laying them flat on the coffee table in front of her. She told Nick the story of how Dominic and Josephine started an affair in Italy. Josephine became pregnant with Lessa and had the baby a couple of years before coming to America. She knew Dominic was the father. Joseph and Josephine had not been close for some time. He was interested in business. In gambling. In drinking and carousing, and not so much in being married. He brought those same priorities across the ocean.

Dominic and Josephine spent plenty of time together on both continents. Back in Italy, when Joseph took off on one of his three-day binges to Rome or Milan, and even longer trips south to the Amalfi coast, Josephine and Dominic would visit the Palazzo del Monte di Pietà in Cento. Dominic marveled at the imaginative architecture of the building itself, its classical emtablatures, while Josephine studied the works of local artists like Zoppo and Gennari. As a little girl, Josephine loved visiting the museums with her mother and imagining her own drawings one day hanging on the consecrated walls beside Michelangelo, da Vinci, Botticelli and the other Masters. When her father, a winemaker, died in 1882 during the grape phylloxera epidemic that destroyed most of the vineyards in Italy and France, her museum outings became few and far between because her days were spent working with her mother cleaning houses or caring for her younger siblings at home. With Dominic she was delighted to relive her childhood fantasies and could even share them with her paramour since he harbored his own appreciation for the arts. On some of their covert excursions they would sit for hours in the Piazza Guercino drinking espresso and discussing art and artists. The inattentive Joseph had absolutely no interest in delving outside his own self-built cultural confines, and neither did he care much about his wife's curiosities.

In Geneva, Dominic and Josephine drank wine and danced late at night in the bar at Morelli's after everybody went to bed. When Josephine wanted to arrange such a rendezvous, she would tell Dominic that she had just brought home a fresh bag of walnuts, and the couple would know to meet in the bar at their prescribed time. If Dominic wanted to propose the meeting, he would mention during the day to Josephine that his supply of walnuts needed to be replenished. Lessa could tell they were in love from Josephine's letters, especially the parts where she reminisced about their secret encounters. They danced closely and quietly to soft, slow songs from the jukebox to be certain they wouldn't wake the people sleeping upstairs on the other side of the large house. This was not the way they danced at Carnival in Cento during the Lenten season, which was twinned with the Carnival of Brazil in Rio. The Carnival music was loud and pulsing, and they danced wildly, yet rhythmically. They marched in parades along the bustling cobblestone streets and wore bright costumes with colorful feathers and beads. They drank grappa uncaringly, and if they had any fear of being recognized should Joseph or one of his goombahs wander into the same celebration, it only revved their adrenaline.

Lessa said that Dominic wrote back from Attica, but Josephine destroyed the letters after reading them so they would not be discovered. Before Dominic died, he gave Josephine's letters to their daughter.

"You found out about this affair when you read the letters?" Nick asked.

"No. My mother told me before she died, before I went to visit him in prison. She wanted me to know who my father was. My real father. You were a baby. It was the same time of your mother's car accident in Ohio. Mama wrote to Dominic that I knew their secret. Dominic loved my father; they were like brothers. But he loved my mother more. She told me they were happy together, even though everything had to be a secret. As soon as Dominic saw me at the prison that day, he figured why I was there instead of Mama. He knew she was sick. She told him in her last letter that she wouldn't see him again. "Take care of our daughter," she wrote. *Prenditi cura di nostra figlia.*

Despite all the details Lessa revealed to Nick about this clandestine romance, it was still hard to believe that it was real, even when he started to piece things together. The prison visits, the way Dominic doted over Lessa, over Edie, Lucky and Buster. His grandmother was a love child. He got that. But how did Dominic and Josephine carry on an affair serious enough to have a child together in total secrecy, and for so long? Under the same roof that Josephine shared with her husband? With her family and closest friends? The back room at Morelli's was an incubator of gossip and insinuation. That room broke more stories in a week than the local newspaper did in a year. No one saw any sign of this affair? Not even their daughter

Lessa who, ironically, referred to Dennis and Nick as "those little bastards" during all their formative years?

"They never told me," Lessa said. "I loved Joseph. I was always his little girl. I was his favorite. He used to put me to bed when I was a baby. And sing to me. He never put my brothers or sister to bed. I'm glad they didn't tell me. It would have broke my heart. It would have broke Joseph's heart too."

"So nobody fucking new?" Nick blurted. He didn't like swearing in front of his grandmother, but this news was hard to swallow.

"One person knew. You didn't know him. He died a long time before you was born."

"Did he die from shock?" It was a long, strange day. Nick was getting silly.

"Don't be a wise guy," Lessa scolded. "He didn't die from shock. He was shot in the head. I think it was in the head. Near the restaurant. They sent Dominic to prison for killing him."

Nick had heard the stories over the years about Dominic going to prison for shooting a man. He thought it was over a card game or a gambling debt. It could have been urban legend for all he knew. But this new information about the love triangle gave the story a new level of credence. And certainly, for Nick, a new level of interest.

"His name was Grillo. Al Grillo," Lessa said. "They was all half-ass friends. Him, Joseph, Dominic. Leone. A bunch of them. Leone was the one who gave the baseball card to Dominic. I bet he wished he never did that."

Nick could not be sure how Mr. Leone would have felt about the Wagner card, what with him being dead for probably thirty years by then. But he figured everybody in Lessa's currently solvent family would not welcome the Leone heirs clamoring for their share of the card's proceeds after so many years. That part of his grandmother's story would stay between them.

"Mama and Dominic were dancing in the bar one night," Lessa explained. "They must have forgot to lock the front door and Al walked in. He was drunk and wanted more to drink. He acted like he didn't see nothin', but the next day he told Dominic he wanted a thousand dollars, or he was going to tell Joseph what he saw. Mama and Dominic dancing close. Kissing. Dominic thought he was bluffing, but Mama didn't think so. She was worried. One night the men were all drinking and playing cards in the bar and Al was shooting off his mouth. Dominic was scared he was gonna say something about him and Mama, so he picked a fight with him over cards, I think, so he could make him go outside. That's when Al got shot."

Nick was processing the story as methodically as he could. "So, you're telling me that Dominic, in order to keep Joseph from finding out about the affair with your mother, killed this Al Grillo guy?" His words came out in a slow and steady cadence with a tinge of sarcasm.

"Dominic didn't kill Al," Lessa said.

"But you told me he went to prison for the murder."

"He did go to prison for the murder. For 21 years. But he didn't kill Al?

"Then who did?"

"Mama. It was Mama who shot Al Grillo that night by the restaurant."

On the night of the shooting in 1935, Josephine heard the two men arguing from her bedroom window above the alley. She knew the confrontation was about the hush money Grillo wanted in exchange for his silence, and she reckoned he would end up either telling her husband about the affair or doing harm to Dominic. Neither outcome she could bear. Dominic did not have a thousand dollars and no way of obtaining it, and Josephine could not have come up with that much money without going to Joseph. She retrieved a thirty-two-caliber pistol hidden in a hat box on the top shelf of her closet, ran down the stairs, out the front door and around the house to the alley where the two men were fighting. Josephine purchased the handgun, which was loaded with six bullets, a few years earlier when Joseph started making regular trips to New York City, usually for three or four days at a time, and she wanted a means to protect herself and her young children from the seedy occupants of the Lehigh Valley train tracks, should the circumstances arise. She had no reason to inform her husband of the acquisition.

Grillo had his blade raised over his head and was about to start slashing Dominic when Josephine fired three shots from her pistol. Two of the shots hit Grillo in the chest, causing him to stagger back a couple of feet but not fall. He was still holding the blade above his head and was again moving toward Dominic. Josephine moved closer to the wounded man and fired two more shots, one again hitting him in the chest, the other in the back as he turned and fell, face down.

She ran to Dominic and they fell into each other's arms. Dominic grabbed the gun from Josephine. She was crying. She was shaking. He wanted to hold her for much longer but knew the men inside the restaurant would soon appear and the police would not be far behind. He told her to run back into the house the same way she came out and to stay there, no matter what happened. "Never talk about this. I love you," Dominic said. *Non parlare mai di questo. Ti amo.* He stuffed the gun in his pocket and ran toward the train tracks.

"Come back to me. I love you," Josephine replied. *Torna da me. Ti amo.*

To Nick, the meteorologist, Lessa's story was the equivalent of an 8.0 magnitude earthquake, 33 times stronger than the 7.0 quakes he had covered a couple times during his career. His great grandmother was an adulterer and a murderer. Even Lizzie Borden could claim only one of the two transgressions. His great grandfather, who he never knew was his great grandfather, did 21 years in the toughest prison this side of Alcatraz for a crime he never committed, even though he could have easily proved his innocence. To top it all off, his dear, sweet Grandma Lessa was a bastard child cloaked in secrecy. "Why," he thought to himself, "am I writing a goddamn cookbook?"

"Dominic must have really loved your mother," Nick said, embarrassed by his own understatement. "He went to prison for 20 years and never killed anyone."

"Oh, he killed a man," Lessa said, casually. "Just not Al Grillo."

"What? Who? Why? When?" In Nick's world, his grandmother's story now registered 9.0 on the Richter scale.

"Nunziato. The cigarette salesman," Lessa said. "You remember him? He stole a lot of money from me. Money I won at the track."

"I remember he was killed on the farm where we used to pick dandelions. Someone pounded a nail into his head. The cops even asked me about him. I saw the body. I puked all over it. Dominic killed him?"

"Yeah."

"How do you know that? I thought the police never found the killer."

"I just know. His friend helped him. A man named LaDuca. He drove the car. They knew he stole money from me. I told them when it happened but swear to God, Nicky, I didn't say to kill him. They did that on their own. I never cared that he got killed. He got what he deserved. But I didn't tell nobody to kill him."

As Lessa was putting the letters back in her jewelry box, Nick, holding his head in his hands, dazed and exhausted, asked: "What's the walnut for?"

"Mama gave it to me to give to Dominic when I went to see him in prison. She said he would understand. I forgot all about it, so I just kept it with the letters."

"Oh yeah, the secret walnut sex code," Nick said. "That reminds me. I'll never eat another walnut without having a revolting carnal thought."

CHAPTER TWENTY
Turkey Meatballs

The last time Nick saw his grandmother alive she had been moved out of her assisted living apartment and into the full-care facility of the nursing home. She had her own room with a bathroom, but no kitchen. There was a bed, a chair, a dresser and a nightstand, all standard issue. She wore a flowered blouse, loose fitting black pants and black orthopedic shoes. The shoemaker in Geneva was always a loyal Morelli's customer, and Lessa would only buy shoes from his store. His name was Russo. Nick was sure these shoes must have come from someone on the Russo family tree. Over her blouse Lessa wore a familiar looking smock. She always wore smocks instead of aprons in the kitchen because the smocks had pockets. The Morelli's smocks were usually stained with tomato sauce and dusted with flour. This one was spotless.

Lessa was sitting in a wheelchair when Nick walked into her room. Her face lit up and she called out to him. "Dennis," she said.

"Nicky, Grandma. I'm Nicky."

She knew exactly who he was, just not by name.

Her eyes were more soulful then Nick remembered. Not sharp and darting like they used to be. She looked tired and fragile. In the halcyon days of the restaurant Lessa was sturdy. Indefatigable. Every morning she would open a dozen No.10 cans of crushed and whole tomatoes with a heavy duty stainless steel can opener that clamped onto the edge of the countertop; slice mounds of garlic; chop a basket of fresh parsley; and carry in a couple cases of bottled milk that had been delivered to the back door, all before she had her first cup of coffee.

When he kissed her on the cheek, Nick could almost smell the sauce simmering on the stove in Morelli's kitchen. Right outside her room the staff was getting ready to serve dinner in the communal dining area, and the clattering of plates and clinking of glasses reminded him of Morelli's kitchen on a Saturday night.

"Are you working, Nicky?"

"Yeah. I'm working Grandma."

"What do you do?

"I'm a weatherman. I tell the weather on TV. In Boston."

"I remember you were writing a cookbook. Did you put me in your cookbook?"

"Of course you're in the cookbook. How could there be a cookbook without you?"

They talked for an hour about the family. She tried to tell Nick where all her other grandchildren – his cousins – were living those days. He knew enough about them to work around her fading recollections and match names with places. But she was in the ballpark.

They talked about food and about Edie, still Lessa's two favorite subjects.

"How's the food here?" Nick asked. "Something out there smells good."

"It's alright. Buster brings me maybe once a week to the Chinese restaurant. I like that. Real Chinese people cook there. I think they came all the way from China. Sometimes I bring back a doggie bag. You ever eat there Nicky? You should go there. Tell Buster I said to bring you."

"What about the food in here? Do they cook Italian?" Nick asked.

"Spaghetti and meatballs, sometimes. The meatballs are too plain. I think they use turkey. And not enough garlic. It's alright."

"Turkey meatballs? That's blasphemy. Why don't you show them how to make Morelli's meatballs?"

"I think they have to cook how the doctors tell them."

TIM DAVIS

"What about the sauce? How's the sauce here?"

"I don't like it so much," Lessa said. "They cook it too fast. They burn it. You should always let the sauce simmer, Nicky. Do you let the sauce simmer?"

CHAPTER TWENTY-ONE

Post Time

Lessa died on a sun-drenched Tuesday. Relatives, friends, acquaintances and even people who had never met her, descended upon Geneva to pay their final respects. Every member of her family that had moved away returned for the services, and they brought with them every member of their own families. Relatives from Italy came to America, some for the first time. Sora Banka returned from Kraków, Poland for the services. She had moved there a few years earlier, after her husband passed away, to live with her cousin Stefania. The trip to Geneva was long and toilsome for Mrs. Banka, who despite using a walker now to get around looked every bit as refined and tasteful as she did on those afternoons when she visited Lessa and Sofia in the back room at Morelli's.

Whammy LaDuca was there to pay his respects. Michael was the first to recognize him as he made his way toward the open casket in the front of the room in a pronounced gait that caused him to lift his leg high enough in stride to keep his foot from dragging on the floor. Michael amused himself with the thought that LaDuca had spent so much time around horses that he had started to walk like one. In fact, LaDuca was suffering from a peroneal nerve palsy, among several other debilitating illnesses, that kept him housebound most of the time. Lessa's wake was his first public appearance in over three months.

Mary Lou Malloy Vogel attended Lessa's wake. She did not know Lessa well but knew that she was kind to her father, who did handy work at the restaurant decades earlier. Whenever Mr. Malloy did a job at Morelli's he would come home with a dinner or a pizza for Mary Lou, and usually a beef bone for her dog, Cha-Cha. When she had her son, Gordy, Jr., Lessa gave Mr. Malloy $100 to send to his daughter in Florida. Gordy, Jr. had a son of his own now, which made Mary Lou the sexiest grandmother Nick had ever seen.

The viewing line in the funeral parlor, the same funeral parlor that buried all the Morellis who predeceased Lessa, extended out the front door and far enough down Pultney Street to cross three intersections, each one managed by a police officer. The normal viewing hours were from six to eight in the evening, but anticipating a larger-than-normal calling, the owners extended the closing time to 9PM. It was near midnight before the last mourner left and the casket was closed for a final time.

The next morning, every pew in Saint Thomas Aquinas church was tightly packed for Lessa's funeral. The parish monsignor said mass and was served by six altar boys, including two of Lessa's great grandchildren and one great nephew. Her firstborn grandson, Dennis Poole, delivered the eulogy. He did not talk about Morelli's, or how his Grandma Lessa held sway over the kitchen. Dennis didn't mention his grandmother's struggle with depression or how she overcame one tragedy after another to keep the business and the family moving forward. Rather, he spoke about the lessons he learned during the year he turned seventeen, the year he obtained his driver's license and became Lessa's de facto chauffeur; he was her only grandchild old enough to drive at the time. He drove her to the produce stand on Route 14 for apples, peaches, watermelons, and freshly picked ears of corn. He took her to the supermarket, to farm fields to pick mushrooms and dandelions, to the department store when she needed new clothes or to buy gifts for family and friends.

Lessa knew that Dennis was not a strong student, in fact he barely passed from one grade to the next through elementary school and did not do any better once he made it to high school. Edie confided in her mother that Dennis might not make it through his senior year, and even if he did, "what kind of job will he end up with?"

"Grades don't tell what kinda person you are," Lessa would say to Dennis on their jaunts. "Lotsa jerks get good grades. Good grades don't mean you gotta be smart. Bad grades don't mean you gotta be stupid. Maybe you ain't smart, Dennis. But you ain't stupid, either. What people see is how hard you work. Just work hard and be honest. Can you do that Dennis? Can you do that?"

While Lessa's lectures on hard work and honesty did little to ease her grandson's existential angst, Dennis did find a certain inspiration in her guidance at the Mare-Do-Well Racetrack, where he drove her twice a week for the better part of the season before he moved to Kentucky. She showed him how to use the daily racing form to choose the horse most likely to win the race. She explained the difference between exactas, quinellas, trifectas and, her favorite of course, daily doubles. Lessa taught him about furlongs, the backstretch and betting "on the nose" versus "show" versus "place." Dennis focused as intently as Dennis could focus – concentration was never among his core competencies — until his grandmother escorted him to the paddock. That's when he lost any interest he pretended to have in the mathematics of horse racing and became completely mesmerized by the horses themselves. Gorgeous, athletic, shiny thoroughbreds with long, powerful legs and flowing manes. They stood upright with heads held high and big bright eyes wide open and observant. Dennis got to know the jockeys, trainers, stable hands. He followed them around the paddock like a rat following the Pied Piper. He learned what the horses ate, how they trained, even how they slept – mostly standing up for normal sleep and lying down for shorter periods when they needed a deeper slumber.

The post-funeral reception and luncheon for Lessa was not a traditional Italian affair. There was no chicken soup with homemade noodles, no rigatoni in dark red tomato sauce, no Ragu. There was no table laden with Italian cookies and cheesecakes and bottles of Anisette, no industrial-sized coffee maker. Lessa's memorial meal was held at The Old Hickory Pit, a Kentucky-style barbeque restaurant located at 59 Lehigh Lane. The buffet included 12-hour smoked pulled pork, beef brisket that fell apart with a fork, and dry rubbed baby back ribs so tender you could practically lick the meat off the bone. There were platters of barbequed ham and turkey, two types of slaw, red potato salad, mashed potatoes with brown gravy, sweet potato casserole, mac-n-cheese, assorted vegetables and corn bread, hush puppies and onion rings. A separate dessert table was loaded with peach cobbler, banana pudding and pecan pie. There were pitchers of sweetened and unsweetened iced tea. It was an open bar with over 15 brands of authentic Kentucky bourbon. The bartenders could not keep up with the demand for Mint Juleps.

Dennis hosted the reception. He bought the building from its post-Morelli's owners for less than they paid – he had become a pretty good horse trader – and opened The Old Hickory Pit the year before Lessa died. He knocked down a couple of walls to create a totally open dining space and decorated it in a southern motif. He left the physical bar intact but added farmhouse-type wooden stools – more casual and arguably less comfortable than the previous seating, but authentic looking. On the men's room door he hung a sign that read "Stallions." On the lady's room "Mares." He kept most of the kitchen appliances, but to expand the cooking space he had to break into the back room, a decision he made with melancholy. He bought a 2,700-pound wood-burning BBQ smoker with three racks for $20,000 from a friend back in Kentucky who built it from scratch, and had it shipped to Geneva for another $900. The smoker was housed in a brick shed behind the restaurant, built exactly on the same spot Lessa once planted her heirloom tomatoes and Italian parsley. Another decision Dennis made dolefully.

During his 15 years in Kentucky, Dennis learned everything he could about three things – horses, barbeque, and bourbon. In his third year on the dude ranch, Dennis took a call from True Bennett, the owner of a large thoroughbred breeding and training farm near Lexington who was looking to sell a few geldings. Dennis got enough information over the phone to recommend to his boss that they bring the horses in for a "look see." Mr. Bennett brought four horses to Lake Barkley and Dennis was tasked with thoroughly examining each. Under Mr. Bennett's scrutinous watch, Dennis checked the bones, joints, tendons, and ligaments of all four horses. He studied their gaits while they walked, trotted, and galloped. He let the horses roam in the pen with the ranch stock to get an idea of their temperaments. He carefully observed their sniffing and nibbling, and how they reacted around their food buckets. The dude ranch was a simple operation without complex testing protocols. Dennis, on his own, would make the call to buy or pass.

"These three are good for the price," Dennis told his boss. "They're smart and trainable. They have good balance and are pretty calm. Nice strait legs." He pointed to the fourth horse. "Not so much this one. He gets spooked too easy. Probably handled quite a bit. Wouldn't be good for new riders. For kids."

Nothing about Dennis's assessment came as a surprise to Mr. Bennett. He had been told that same thing about the fourth horse by a professional trainer with many years of experience and access to sophisticated testing methods, but nevertheless figured he could find the horse a home on a simple dude ranch. Mr. Bennett was so impressed with Dennis's natural equine instincts that while he was in the office wrapping up the deal with John, the dude ranch owner, he asked about Dennis's availability.

"Well, lemme see," John answered with a chin scratch. "He's on the clock til six, and I don't believe he's working in the kitchen tonight. I think we're bringing in pizzas. Yup, it's pizza night. So, I guess he's free after six. But I gotta tell you. He thought he knocked up my niece once, so I don't guess he swings your way. But hey, give it a go. It's a free country. Lord knows the boy could use a night on the town."

"What? No. That's not ..." Mr. Bennett was shocked, but then told himself he shouldn't be. "Look, I'd like to offer him a job ... on my farm ... you know, working with horses. I wanted to make sure you're OK with that."

John looked dazed, and embarrassed. While he was fumbling for something to say, Mr. Bennett spoke up. "I'll give you all four horses for the price of two if you let me offer Dennis a job. You can keep the horses at that price even if he doesn't come to work for me." Mr. Bennett was confident he could make Dennis an offer that he'd be hard pressed to turn down. He thought Dennis would relish the idea of working with serious horses rather than a herd of hand-me-downs.

"Deal," John exclaimed. "I'm gonna miss that boy. But I can use those horses. Even that one Dennis says is crazy. Hell, he might not even take the job. Got it pretty good here, ya know."

Dennis jumped at the job offer. It was his chance to work with thoroughbreds, the kind of horses that captivated him summers ago at the Mare-Do-Well racetrack. Mr. Bennett's offer included a free room at the breeding farm, all his meals and more money than he was making at the dude ranch. It was a no-brainer. The day he left, John told him he could always come back to the ranch, maybe even some day as the head wrangler. It was a comforting notion for Dennis but, in his mind, he would be gone for good.

After a one-week orientation at the True-ly Thoroughbred Breeding Farm in Midway, Kentucky, Mr. Bennett assigned Dennis to work with two of the younger horses, a job normally reserved for more experienced handlers and trainers. He was mentored by Peter Dutko, a real-life cowboy who was born on a horse ranch, raised on a horse ranch, and worked on a horse ranch every day since he was ten. "Horses like predictable," Dutko told Dennis on their first day together. "They want to know what's coming, when it's coming, how it's coming. They don't like surprises. Not just when they're training in the pen. Every time you are with your horse, you are training him. Remember that. He'll let you know what works and what doesn't work. Pay attention. He'll train you as much as you train him."

In his first few months on the job Dennis learned some hard and painful lessons, like not to kiss a horse that has a toothache, especially one whose teeth are long and sharp. He'll have that reminder on his right cheek for as long as he lives. Another time he noticed a horse whose head bobbing was becoming increasingly intense, so he tried a harsher bit. He was immediately thrown clear out of the pen and landed ass first on the working end of a pitchfork. His reminder this time wound up on his other right cheek, along with a scar from eight stitches.

"Goddamn it Dennis," Dutko yelled, doing his best not to smile. "That horse is telling you he doesn't like all them skeeters flying round his ears. That's why he's tossing his head. It ain't got nothing to do with the damn bit. Try listening more and thinking less."

"I didn't hear the damn horse say anything," Dennis said under his breath. "Seven hundred acres of beautiful bluegrass and I land on a fucking fork."

Over the next 15 years Dennis proved to be a very talented and successful trainer of thoroughbred racehorses. He not only learned how to accurately diagnose a problem with a horse, but also how to understand what caused the problem to begin with. His rate of wastage during the training and racing of his horses was the lowest in the history of the True-ly Farm, and its owner, True Bennett, paid him handsomely for his expertise, as well as for his performance at the track. In 51 starts Dennis had a Kentucky Derby winner, a Preakness winner, and many first and second place finishers at major tracks around the country, including Santa Anita Park in California and Saratoga in New York. The horses he trained earned True-ly over seven million dollars and helped him salt away a healthy nest egg for himself.

In 1994 Dennis retired from True-ly and moved back to Geneva with a scar on each of his right cheeks, a wad of cash including a generous exit bonus from Mr. Bennett, and a taste for horse racing, Kentucky barbeque and authentic bourbon. Since he wouldn't be happy without his barbeque and bourbon, he opened The Old Hickory Pit in the former Morelli's. His food menu included the most popular dishes from his favorite barbeque joints in Lake Barkley and Lexington and all the pits in between. His list of bourbons came directly from the Kentucky Bourbon Trail, where he spent much of his free time trolling the distilleries sampling the classics. His favorite was the award-winning eight-year-old Buffalo Trace Kentucky Straight Bourbon from the Buffalo Trace Distillery on the Kentucky River in Frankfort, Kentucky.

Dennis bought a small farm on the outskirts of Geneva, and before he even furnished the bedroom he purchased two fillies at auction. At Lessa's post funeral reception, Dennis was standing at the bar with his brothers, Nick and Joe, cousin Michael and uncle Buster. They were sipping their small batch Buffalo Trace bourbon and perusing that day's Racing Form from the Mare-Do-Well Racetrack. One horse in the second race was circled in pencil:

"Lessa's Legacy. Owner: Dennis Poole. Trainer: Dennis Poole."

The end

Epilogue

Over the years The Old Hickory Pit has provided steady and gainful summer employment for school-aged Morelli descendants. Like their parents and grandparents, they haul crates of produce and boxes of meats into walk-in coolers. They carry heavy cans of condiments, six to a case, down a steep, creaky set of wooden steps to the small basement below the kitchen. They lift commercial size containers of ice cream and other frozen desserts into giant freezers. And they hump buckets of ice from the basement below the bar to the wells behind the bar. Only now, it's a much more pleasant job. The once dark, dank basement is routinely painted in pastel shades. Bright lights have been installed throughout the space, and the switch was moved to the top of the steps from the bottom. Best of all, the grouchy, old ice machine that once frightened its callers with its loud and sudden bursts, has been replaced by a four-hundred-pound state-of-the-art ice machine with foam insulated bins and user-friendly easy-touch screen controls. The machine can produce 550 pounds of ice per day, with each cube consistently measuring seven-eighths of an inch on every side. The cubes are larger than normal, so they melt more slowly and water down drinks less, something Dennis insists upon so as not to dilute his precious Kentucky bourbons.

Dennis, never a wiz at math – or any of the other elementary school core subjects, for that matter – is a more than admirable bookkeeper for his restaurant. He never misses an entry and his bank account is always in good stead. With his suppliers he is tough but fair; he is eager to try new items but never overspends his budget; and he pays his bills on time with official Old Hickory Pit business checks decorated with a montage of popular bourbon labels. He paid a little extra just to have use of the trademarks.

The Old Hickory Pit has a very loyal following. The prices are reasonable even though it is the only barbeque joint for miles around. The food is always cooked and served fresh; the service is familiar and warm. Despite its location in the "ass end" of the town, most nights are filled to capacity. Dennis offers to pay cab fare for any patron who enjoys the bourbon to excess.

Occasionally, Dennis and the family members still around get a hankering for a homecooked Italian meal, and they reminisce about Lessa, Sofia, Gus and all the people who came and went at 59 Lehigh Lane in the days when it housed Morelli's Restaurant. When that happens, they merely pour their favorite drinks and toast to the portrait that hangs on the wall between the bar and the dining room. The portrait with the gold plate on the bottom of the frame with the inscription:

Joseph and Josephine Morelli
Founders
Morelli's Restaurant

After Words

The story you have just read really did start out as a cookbook in honor of my late mother, Adelaide "Addie" Davis (March 11, 1929 – November 13, 1994), a truly world class chef and an amazing mother and human being. Rest in peace, Mom.

But somewhere between Alfredo and Zuppa, my imagination got the better of me.

This is a novel, a fictional presentation. Like most novels it is rooted in some perception of the truth, but for the most part this novel is purely a product of my imagination and intuition. Any historical reference or resemblance to characters and events is merely for story-telling purposes, and by no means intended to set straight any actual accounts.

The real Geneva, New York is on a beautiful freshwater lake with a unique macroclimate that makes it an ideal home to a bunch of wineries. It's "The Lake Trout Capital of the World." Lake trout are delicious deep fried, pan fried, baked or broiled. Imagine a meal of fresh-caught lake trout served with coleslaw, salt potatoes and garlic bread, and topped off with homemade apple pie made with apples from one of the area's thriving orchards.

There's a collegiate level baseball team in Geneva, dozens of outstanding restaurants – family-owned and popular chains, a state-of-the-art New York State Agricultural Experiment Station – a division of Cornell University, and a prestigious homegrown college – Hobart and William Smith. Every summer the town hosts a National Lake Trout Derby and a Cruisin' Night featuring a parade of classic cars. Both occasions attract people from miles around.

You'd be hard-pressed to find a better place to spend a summer weekend than Geneva, New York. Try the lake trout.

Acknowledgements

I would like to thank the following people for their help in checking the technical accuracy of certain material in this novel:

Austin Muldoon, retired New York Police Department (NYPD) Detective, who was instrumental in helping me correctly describe the murder, arrest, trial and sentencing sequence as it relates to the homicide that took place in 1935.

Dr. Mervyn Lloyd, MD FRCS Orthopaedic Surgeon, for his direction and consultation in the section of this novel related to Edie Poole's left leg surgery and recovery following the 1955 automobile accident.

Richard Lecky, for his help in describing the military career of his father – Hugh F. Lecky, Jr. – the "Heli Padre."

Last but certainly not least, thanks to **Bruce Crilly** for his beautiful cover design on this book. I worked with Bruce for many years and his artistic talents always made my writing seem better. He is a pro's pro.

About the author

Tim Davis was born in 1955 in Geneva, NY and lived there for the first 18 years of his life. He graduated from Bowling Green State University in Ohio in 1977 with a bachelor's degree in journalism and has been writing ever since. He cut his teeth in the consumer press in New York City in 1977. From there he went to work for a series of business magazines covering various fields to include beverages, retail, video, audio, and even frozen foods – pretty much everything but the kitchen sink. Although he did write about home furnishings for a time.

During his 40-plus-year career as a journalist, writer and editor, Mr. Davis has interviewed many captains of global industry; written for and about some of the world's most iconic companies and brands; helped both his children pen their college essays; and authored hundreds of touching and witty birthday, anniversary and Valentine notes to his wife.

Throughout his life, the author has been an avid fan and participant of many sports. His athletic pursuits these days are limited primarily to golf, which explains the passage about the 1956 U.S. Open Golf Championship in "Let the sauce simmer." The account in the novel about the Honus Wagner baseball card was drawn from Mr. Davis' own experience as a collector from 1965 to 1975 which, unfortunately, coincided precisely with the "lean years" of his beloved NY Yankees. His collection included the likes of Horace Clarke, Tom Tresh, Jerry Kenney and Jake Gibbs. He was not at all disappointed when his mother sold the house he grew up in with all its contents, including his unexceptional card collection. She also sold his dog, which he missed more than his card collection.

Despite enduring the worst decade in the history of the NY Yankees, Mr. Davis remains a diehard Yankees fan, and he has been abundantly rewarded for his loyalty and patience. He attended several of the team's World Series games since 1977, including his favorite: Game 6 in 1977 at Yankee Stadium where Reggie Jackson hit three home runs.

On July 4, 1983, Dave Righetti became the first Yankee since Don Larsen in 1956 to throw a no-hitter. Mr. Davis had a field level seat to the game. He never made it. Instead his girlfriend "convinced" him to accompany her to the beach on that gorgeous 94-degree day. She did not remain his girlfriend much longer. On June 16, 1984, she became his wife. They've been happily married ever since, and she never again talked him out of attending a Yankees game.

Mr. Davis currently resides in Montvale, NJ with his wife Helene. They have two children, Danielle and Sam. They are both grown and on their own. Mr. Davis has three siblings: Bill, Lisa and Steve. They are also grown and on their own.

One more thing: As a schoolboy the author worked very briefly bussing tables in his family's restaurant. He was not very good at it. His own mother fired him. Really.

If you enjoyed "Let the Sauce Simmer," please submit a review via any of the on-line bookseller sites.

Food for thought

A taste of Mom's cooking

These are a few of my favorite dishes that Mom made for us. I chose these because they are, what I call, "makeable." They are relatively easy to prepare and most of the ingredients are probably already somewhere in your kitchen or certainly within the aisles of any supermarket. There is nothing fancy or "nouveau" about these dishes. We would not have had them any other way.

BEST EVER MARINATED FLANK STEAK

I love flank steak. You could cook it on top of a grass fire and it would taste great. But the way my mother made it for us was sensational. She would whip up some mashed potatoes and use the pan drippings thickened with homemade roux to make gravy. Dinner is served.

- one small onion chopped
- one clove garlic minced
- third cup dry sherry
- quarter cup soy sauce
- one-and-a-half tablespoon honey
- one tablespoon olive oil
- one teaspoon Worcestershire Sauce

195

- quarter teaspoon ground ginger
- quarter teaspoon pepper

Combine all and stir til smooth. Place steak in shallow pan and cover with marinade. Refrigerate at least 12 hours. Broil or grill til desired wellness.

RIGATONI IN VODKA CREAM SAUCE
As a little girl, my daughter Danielle would order Penne in Vodka Cream Sauce every time we went out to dinner. On one such occasion Mom told her she could make it better. She may have had this recipe long before Danielle was even born, but Mom told her she created it just for her. Danielle loved it. Still does.

- one tablespoon butter
- one clove garlic
- Prosciutto (Mom did not include an amount)
- one tomato peeled and chopped
- quarter cup vodka
- one cup heavy cream

Sauté garlic in butter. Add tomato and cook 5 minutes. Add vodka and cook 2 minutes. Add cream and cook 5 minutes. Mix with cooked rigatoni. Mom's pasta was always al dente.

APPLE BROWN BETTY
Our favorite dessert. Served warm in a bowl with milk poured over, or with vanilla ice cream. A fixture every Fall in Geneva. I have no idea what kind of apples Mom used even though I'm sure I helped pick them, despite my whining.

- one quart apples (about 7)
- half teaspoon lemon juice
- two tablespoons flour

- half cup sugar
- quarter cup room temp butter
- half cup brown sugar
- half cup oatmeal
- quarter cup flour

Mix apples, lemon juice, flour, sugar together in bowl. In separate bowl mix butter, brown sugar, oatmeal, flour til crumbly. Spread over apple mixture. Bake 350 deg 40 to 45 min. Check midway.

PASTA PUTTANESECA

My mother told me that Puttaneseca means "prostitute" in Italian. I looked it up. The Italian word for prostitute is "Putana." I don't care. Puttaneseca is the most flavorful of all Italian sauces. Hell, if you rubbed capers, olives, and anchovies on a dead squirrel it would have to taste pretty good.

- one pound penne or any pasta
- half cup EVOO (Extra Virgin Olive Oil – is there any other kind?)
- two cloves garlic minced
- quarter teaspoon – or more – crushed hot red pepper
- 28oz can San Marzano plum tomatoes, drained and chopped
- six anchovies lightly rinsed and chopped
- half cup oil-cured black olives pitted and chopped
- one tablespoon capers, one tablespoon capers juice
- chopped fresh basil or parsley, or oregano leaves – no stems

Cook pasta al dente. In skillet sauté garlic in oil til tender, not brown. Stir in hot pepper. Add tomato and anchovies, heat to boil. Simmer 10 minutes until thick. Add olives, capers, herbs. Simmer sauce til thick and fragrant. Add sauce to pasta and toss.

"THIS-IS-NOT-YOUR-MOTHER'S" TUNA FISH SALAD

It's __my__ mother's Tuna Fish Salad. It's worth the extra steps. You'll be the envy of the lunchroom with this working-class sangy.

- large can solid white packed tuna
- one-and-a-half stalks celery, fine chopped
- one medium onion, fine chopped
- tablespoon salt
- couple shakes Cayenne pepper
- about three-and-a half-tablespoon mayonnaise
- couple shakes Paprika
- pimentos sliced thin, to taste

Use a food processor to make the tuna fine. Mix well all ingredients in bowl except mayonnaise and pimentos. Then add pimentos and mayonnaise and mix. Put in fridge to chill. Serve between two slices of white bread with a couple leaves of cold iceberg lettuce.

DESSERT LASAGNA

Any lasagna is a great lasagna. But a Dessert Lasagna is fantastico. This was one of Mom's "go-to" party dishes. Too simple to be so good.

- one box graham crackers
- two 3oz packages instant vanilla pudding mix
- three cups milk
- 8oz container frozen whipped topping thawed
- 16oz package prepared chocolate frosting

Line bottom of 9in x 13in pan with third of graham crackers. In large bowl combine pudding mix and milk. Mix well. Stir whipped topping into putting mixture. Spread half of mixture over layer of graham crackers. Top with another third of graham crackers and the remaining pudding. Top all with final layer of graham crackers.

Warm chocolate frosting in microwave for 30 seconds and pour over graham crackers. Refrigerate at least 5 hours and serve.

CRAB-STUFFED CHICKEN BREASTS

Mom was not above asking for a recipe from someone if she really liked the dish. But she always gave proper credit by writing the person's name on her recipe card. If the recipe came from a magazine or newspaper, she gave credit as well. This one is from Bonnie Jenkins, Mom's good friend for many years. Ms. Jenkins must have been a fine cook in her own right because Mom had several of her recipes in her collection.

- six chicken breasts skinned and boned
- half cup chopped onion
- half cup chopped celery
- three tablespoon butter
- five tablespoons dry white wine
- 7.5oz. can crab meat, drained and flaked
- half cup herb-seasoned stuffing mix
- two tablespoons flour
- half teaspoon paprika
- one envelope Hollandaise sauce mix
- three-quarters cup milk
- half cup shredded Swiss cheese

Pound chicken to flatten. Sprinkle with salt and pepper. Cook onion and celery in butter til tender. Remove from heat and add 3 tablespoons wine, crab, stuffing mix and toss. Divide mixture and spread on breasts. Roll up and secure with toothpicks or tie with twine. Combine flour and paprika and coat chicken. Put in baking dish and drizzle with 2 tablespoons melted butter. Bake uncovered 375 deg. for 1 hr. Transfer to platter. Blend sauce mix and milk, cook and stir til thick. Add remaining 2 tablespoons wine and cheese and stir till cheese melts. Pour some on chicken and pass the rest.

CPSIA information can be obtained
at www.ICGtesting.com
Printed in the USA
BVHW031448131220
595622BV00009B/89

9 781489 730855